NO LITTLE CHOICES

A novel based on a true story

Erin Walsh Hardesty

&

Michael Blass

ISBN: 0692771204
ISBN-13: 978-0692771204 (No Little Choices, LLC)

PRINTED IN THE UNITED STATES OF AMERICA

Cover design by Matt Potter.

This book is a combination of facts about Erin Hardesty's life and certain embellishments. Names, dates, places, events, and details have been changed, invented, and altered for literary effect. The reader should not consider this book anything other than a work of literature.

DEDICATION

For SJM and MEO, who both made excellent choices throughout their entire lives.

Not flesh of my flesh
Not bone of my bone
But still miraculously my own
Never forget for a single minute
You didn't grow under my heart but in it.

—Author Unknown

CONTENTS

CHAPTER 1

1953

The creaking of the stairs under the weight of her stepfather spoke to Quinn O'Connell, whispering that sleep would not come quickly tonight. The dim light sliced the room as her bedroom door opened and quickly retreated as the door closed. She heard his clothes drop into a pile on the floor, and soon he was pulling back the blankets and sliding next to her. He smelled of sweat, tobacco, and Falstaff beer.

He said nothing as he slid his hand to her pajama pants and roughly removed them. She had learned that giving him what he wanted when he wanted it was the easiest and only way. He had taught her long ago that her resistance was futile and easily overcome.

In complete and utter silence, except for his inconsistent breathing, he forced himself upon her small, thirteen-year-old, half-naked body as she dutifully opened her legs. Clenching her eyes closed, she waited for him to enter her. And he did, as he always did, and she endured, as she always endured. He labored rhythmically, oblivious to her discomfort and disconnection. His motions were as much mechanical as animalistic.

She floated to the ceiling and looked down, watching two people but feeling nothing.

He was soon finished.

When she felt his weight shift off of her and out of the bed, she opened her eyes. The darkness of the room was slightly less now than before, as there was enough light from the window for her to make out his movements as he pulled on his pants.

"You need to go to confession." His voice pierced the darkness.

It was the same scene with the same scripted lines each time. This was Sonny's private theater, and she was in a supporting role.

"Yes, I know." Quinn had learned her part and played it flawlessly for what had become a very long run.

"It's between you, the priest, and God. Nobody else. God helps those who help themselves."

The door opened and closed, and she was alone in the room once again. On this night, sleep came late, morning came early, and the transition was not tranquil.

CHAPTER 2

"Dinner will be ready in ten minutes." Grandma Foote glanced over her shoulder at Quinn as the chicken sizzled and popped in the black iron skillet. Clouds of steam from two pots ascended like white, lazy geysers and disappeared into the ceiling as the aged gas stove labored under the watchful eye of its master.

As the warm aroma of peace, place, and provision enveloped her, Quinn quietly assembled the proper place settings on the small wooden table concealed under a plain, cream-colored, cotton tablecloth. Fork on the left. Knife and spoon on the right, napkin folded and to the left of the fork, the light-green opaque dinner plate in the center. Water glass above and to the right of the plate. Quinn knew Grandma never altered her table-setting routine, even when she was dining alone, as was frequently the case.

Grandma Foote was one who ran her quaint home with military efficiency. She deployed routine and structure to prevail against the twin enemies of chaos and clutter. Yet here, Quinn felt more at home than anywhere else. She had lived with Grandma off and on for the past seven years, ever since her dad died when she was six years old.

"Quinn, any idea what happened this time?" Grandma asked softly as they settled into their appointed positions at the table.

"I came home from school yesterday and heard them yelling when I walked in the house. They stopped as soon as I walked in, but Mom looked at me and told me I was going to come live with you again for a while." Quinn looked into the kind, brown eyes of her grandmother.

"I see," Grandma said, reaching across the table and patting Quinn's hand lightly. "Well, you and I will be just fine here, and we'll let it blow over with those two."

Quinn nodded and changed the subject. "Say, Grandma, I heard some chirping out on your porch and saw a bird's nest up on the ledge by the ceiling."

"Those robins. They build a nest there every year. If you heard the chirping, then they've hatched. I've noticed the mama bird coming and going quite a bit. She must be feeding them constantly."

"When I walked closer, I found a baby bird lying on the floor of the porch, all alone," Quinn said.

"Dead or alive?" Grandma asked.

"Alive"

"Is it still there?"

"No, I put it back in the nest."

"Oh, Quinnie," Grandma said, "you ought not have done that. The mother likely pushed the bird out of the nest to make room for the others."

Quinn stopped eating. "But why would she do that? The little baby will die!"

"Well, the mother knows if one of her babies is different than the others, it needs to be removed so the other stronger babies can survive. It's okay. It's nature's way."

Quinn thought for a moment. "Since I put it back in the nest, what will the mother do?"

Grandma swallowed her bite. "I suppose she will either not feed the baby or, more likely, push it out again. Either way, it is not likely to survive."

"It doesn't seem fair, Grandma."

"It's life, Quinn. Fair is something involving a pig and a blue ribbon."

Quinn quietly finished her dinner, contemplating this great injustice. Once done, she rose to help Grandma with the dishes. As Grandma washed, Quinn dried the dishes and put them away.

"Grandma, if that bird gets pushed out again, I want to try to help it."

"Are you still thinking about that crazy bird, Quinnie?" Grandma's eyebrows arched slightly as she inspected Quinn's face, her hands submerged in dishwater. She thought for a minute as she scrubbed the black skillet, the last of the dishes and the most stubborn to clean.

"Okay, but you can't remove the bird from the nest. You have to wait for the mother to push it out. If it survives the fall, then you can try to save it," she said with a matter-of-factness that always penetrated the room once she had made up her mind. "But I want you to keep in mind that it's not likely to survive the next fall. And if it does, you probably can't save it. Understand?"

"Yes," Quinn replied softly, unable to conceal a smile.

Quinn quickly finished in the kitchen and went to the porch. There, she found the bird again on the floor, alive and chirping. She was sad yet excited.

"What a tough, little bird you are," she mumbled and slowly bent to pick it up. Quinn hated that mama bird, which was making quite a racket with another bird in the large oak tree beside the porch.

Grandma appeared at her side with a small, wooden box, retrieved from the cellar. The lidless box was empty.

"We'll need to find some sticks and grass and maybe newspaper to shred up and put in here to keep the bird warm," Grandma instructed. "We also need a few worms and bugs to feed the little critter."

Quinn gently placed the bird in the box and left him on the back stoop of the house while she and Grandma scoured the yard for the necessary, lifesaving measures. Soon they had constructed a nest of sorts inside the box and dug up a few worms, which Quinn gently dropped into the outstretched mouth of the tiny robin.

"Grandma, I think he's going to be fine. Now he's got a home and food and all we have to do is feed him until he's big enough to fly."

"Perhaps, but don't underestimate how hard it may be to keep him fed. If he's not meant to survive, he just won't."

"Can I keep him in my room tonight?"

"Of course not!" Grandma protested. "No wild creatures are living in my house!" Her expression softened as she studied the bird. "I'll tell you what, Quinn. You can put him on the back porch—but that's as far as he gets into my house, understand?"

"Yes, thank you!" She gave her grandmother a quick hug.

Quinn perched the box with the protesting, fuzzy, baby bird on the bench inside the enclosed back porch. With the coming of spring, the days were getting warmer but the nights were still cool, so here he would be safe from the night's chill and the neighborhood cats. Quinn was satisfied and felt an odd and inexplicable joy when she thought about the bird.

For the next several days, Quinn was on bird-feeding duty in the afternoons after school. Grandma, reluctantly, had agreed to feed the bird while Quinn was at school. The little bird grew quickly, and it seemed to change noticeably with each passing day. For Quinn, life was momentarily calm and peaceful as she, the bird, and Grandma set about their daily predictable routines.

CHAPTER 3

"What do you mean, you don't know?" Roxanna glared at her daughter.

Quinn stared blankly back at her mother.

Grandma looked up at her daughter, slowly turned to her granddaughter and then back again at her daughter, her eyes probing Roxanna. The face she'd known since childbirth, affixed to the person she never completely understood. She decided against saying anything.

"Quinn, answer my question!" Roxanna leaned forward in her chair, the wooden table separating the three people in Grandma's tiny kitchen.

"I don't know," Quinn repeated her earlier answer.

Roxanna saw defiance in her daughter's eyes; she was incapable of interpreting Quinn's answer any other way. She looked at her mother, arched her eyebrows slightly while cocking her head to the side and jutting her jaw out.

Grandma saw pain in Quinn's big, dark eyes.

"Roxie, maybe not now, huh?" Grandma's voice was quiet, level, and calm, almost soothing, as if the only two people in the universe at that moment were Grandma and her irate daughter.

Grandma was adept at dealing with Roxanna's outbursts, as she had always been a difficult child subject to the heat of emotion. Roxanna was like her father—God rest his soul—in that regard. Quick to anger, but unlike her father, she was slow to leave the anger behind her, preferring to club her opponent with it in order to get her way. She certainly lacked subtlety and, when she was angry, she lacked self-control. Some people could show anger with a dramatic flair that at least made you appreciate their ability to use it artistically. Not Roxanna. It could be said that she didn't use anger—it used her. She burned hot with it, usually out of proportion to the situation at hand, especially when it came to Quinn.

"What do you mean, 'not now'?" Roxanna retorted. "If not now, when? I want to know who the father of this baby is. I want to get to the bottom of this. Now!" She fixed her gaze upon her pregnant teenager. "How could you not know? How many boys have you been with?" Roxanna spat the words at Quinn. "*How-could-you-do-this?*"

Those words echoed as they seeped corrosively into Quinn's consciousness. She felt her face flush. Her cheeks and ears burned, and she wanted to vomit. But she knew it would only make things worse, prolonging her mother's tirade. She resolved she would not tell. Ever.

"How could you do this to us? You've shamed our family." Roxanna slapped her hand on the table and sat back in her chair. She reached for a cigarette and paused before lighting it.

Quinn knew only the cigarette stood between her face and her mother's quick hands, hands that could slap at the drop of a hat. But through a lifetime of studying such things, Quinn also knew her mother wouldn't slap her while she was smoking. It wasn't clear to Quinn why this was, and it didn't matter. It was one of those things in life that just is, so it becomes part of your world and you deal with it.

"You may think you're a real dolly, but I've got news for you, little girl. You aren't ready to be a grown-up woman yet." Roxanna sucked in a quick breath. "What do you think? You can just get whatever you want by sleeping around? That's what trash does, Quinn, trash!"

Quinn looked down at the table in front of her, hearing but not listening any longer. She thought of the bird and wanted to go see if he was okay. She knew it was inevitable he would soon fly away, leaving her alone.

"Listen to me!" Roxanna spit out her words. "This isn't over. By any means. Go to your room while I talk to Grandma."

Quinn was relieved to be paroled from the kitchen. She shot a glance at Grandma, whose kind eyes reached out, caressed her face, and quietly reassured her. It was in this private space between them where Quinn found solace. Sometimes the space was filled with words, sometimes with a look, but always with the full, unconditional Grandma love that is unlike any other love in the universe.

"Quinn, before you go to your room, will you go check on the bird for me?" Grandma had read her mind. She had a way of doing that.

"Bird? What bird?" Roxanna looked at her mother, then at Quinn, but Quinn was already heading out the door to the back porch. She knew not to stay in her mother's presence unnecessarily.

"Quinn and I've been nursing a baby bird for the past ten days."

Grandma looked at Roxanna. "It's going to fly soon."

"That's the dumbest thing I've ever heard." Roxanna took a pull on her cigarette while eyeballing her mother. Her disdain hung in the room, competing for space above their heads with Roxanna's swirling cigarette smoke.

"Perhaps, but Quinn has proven remarkably committed to feeding that little bird and cares for it every day," Grandma said.

"Well, it's all for nothing," Roxanna replied. "Soon that bird will be gone, and then what will she have? Nothing. What's the point?"

Grandma studied her daughter for a moment as Roxanna stared into space while puffing on her cigarette. The silence between them was common and familiar but never comfortable. It was a wall Grandma scaled at great effort, only to reveal a bleak life within a bleak landscape. But that bleak life was someone important, someone she loved, someone who seemed intent and content to suckle from the barren teat of bleakness for whatever sustenance could be had in such a dark place. Why couldn't Roxanna understand there is a better way, a better world, a better life on the other side of that wall? If only she would make an attempt to climb it or tear it down. But Grandma knew this would never come to pass, so time and again she did the hard climbing and learned to expect very little.

"Listen, Roxanna, I have an idea." Grandma scaled the wall and peered over it.

"What's that?" Roxanna eyed her mother suspiciously.

"Quinn should be sent away to have this baby." Grandma paused and shifted her weight in her seat slightly.

"Yeah, so?"

"So, I was thinking she should go live with Peggy and Howard and have the baby in Norfolk." She stopped talking and watched her daughter writhing in her bleakness.

"No … well, maybe. I'm not saying yes or no. I need to think about this." Roxanna looked away.

"You should think about it, sure. But if she stays here she will be a public spectacle," Grandma continued, not ready to leave her spot atop the wall just yet. "If she lives with your sister, she will be in a good environment, she can have the baby and then come back here and get back in school."

Roxanna butted her cigarette out in the ashtray and folded her arms across her chest.

"Do you think Peggy and Howard would agree?" Roxanna's sudden question surprised her mother.

"Yes, I know they would."

"I need to talk to Sonny. We're going to have to pay for this somehow."

Grandma avoided showing any reaction to the mention of Sonny's name. Roxanna's second husband was part of the reason Roxanna acted the way she did, Grandma was certain of it. There was something about him she didn't like or trust, and she felt it from the day she first met him four years ago. She never shared her feelings with anyone, but she knew Roxanna could sense it.

"Pay for what?" Grandma asked.

"Hospital bills, room and board, I don't know…" Roxanna's voice trailed off, her irritation seeping back to the surface.

"I think if you place the baby for adoption, the hospital bills are covered," Grandma replied, "and Howard and Peggy probably wouldn't take any money if you offered it. You know they love Quinn, and she is so good with their little ones."

Roxanna stood up. "I don't know. I'll call you tomorrow." She turned on her heel and left the house, disappearing into her bleak world and leaving Grandma alone atop the wall.

CHAPTER 4

"If you don't let it go soon, Quinn," Grandma put her hands on Quinn's shoulders and looked into her eyes, "it will die on that back porch. Birds are meant to be free."

Quinn dropped her head and stared at the floral pattern on her grandma's housedress. She tried to speak, but her throat choked down the words. Grandma pulled Quinn's tiny body into her own and hugged her tightly.

"I know, I know," Grandma whispered soothingly, "but this is the right thing. It's the only chance this little creature has to survive."

"But, but," Quinn sputtered, "it wasn't right for the mother to abandon this baby. I hate that mother bird!"

"Oh, Quinnie," Grandma squeezed Quinn a little tighter, "life is full of circumstances and events that don't make sense to us in the moment. Sometimes life hurts, honey."

"But why?"

Grandma straightened up and held Quinn at arm's length while she once again looked in her face. "Why? Sometimes nobody knows *why*, so instead you have to think *how*."

"What? How? I don't understand." Quinn felt confused and slightly irritated.

"Look, sometimes you must forget all about why something is the way it is and start thinking about how you are going to deal with it. Spending too much time worrying about why just distracts you from dealing with how. There comes a point when you have to get on with life, Quinn."

"But ... it's hard."

"Yes, it is. But that is part of growing up. Some things cannot be changed, and you must accept them as they are and move on."

Quinn didn't say anything as she contemplated Grandma's words. This was a lot to think about, and she wanted to scream and stomp her feet and break something.

"Quinn, let's go set the bird free and get it over with."

"But he can't fly yet. How will he survive out there with cats and dogs that can eat him?" Quinn wasn't ready to let anything go yet.

"Do you think he will learn to fly on my back porch?" Grandma asked.

"No, I guess not."

"Let's put him in the box on a low branch in the big evergreen in the backyard," Grandma suggested, "and then let nature take its course. That's the best you can do for him."

With little fanfare and many tears, Quinn bid the bird goodbye as her trembling hands carefully placed the box containing the chirping, clumsily-flopping bird deep into the branches of the broad Douglas fir in Grandma's backyard. Her body was a cauldron for her anger, confusion, and grief, and in that moment she hated everything in the world. Everything except that bird. She even hated Grandma, the one person who could have made this different. Grandma always fixed everything and made everything okay, but now she decided to quit helping.

Quinn stood staring at the tree, waiting for something, anything, good to happen, although she didn't knew what. Quinn wished she could fly so she could soar right out of here—away from Grandma, her mother, Sonny, this bird, everything.

Why does life have to be so hard? I'm sure Grandma is wrong. She's just a crazy, old woman who doesn't know what it's like to be young. What does she know about any of this anyway? Quinn's tears ran silently down her cheeks, the hot by-product of her simmering anger and the grief of being betrayed by Grandma.

"Quinn," a familiar but suddenly peculiar voice called to her from behind.

She turned to see Grandma standing a little distance behind her. Something was different, strange about her grandma in this moment. *What was wrong? Why was she different? What's happened? Why was she standing that way? No that isn't it; is it the way she's holding her head? What's wrong with her voice? Why isn't she saying anything else?* Quinn's mind searched for an explanation.

She walked toward the old woman. And then she saw it, something she had never seen before, and it shocked her and scared her, and she felt like her heart would beat out of her chest.

Tears. On Grandma's cheeks. Tears running from red-rimmed eyes, in perfectly straight parallel lines atop her strong, expressionless face, past her prominent jaw line, onto her neck, and disappearing into her bosom. She stood ramrod straight, as she always did, a picture of strength—but only from a distance.

Quinn was shocked at the sight of a grown woman crying and frightened it was her grandma. She didn't know this strong woman could cry or even did cry. Suddenly, she felt an overwhelming sense of love for her grandma, and in that moment, inexplicably, she thought of the bird and her grandma and felt a rush of love for them both.

"Grandma!" Quinn flung her arms around the worn-out, aged woman.

"Quinnie," Grandma whispered to her, "sometimes life just overtakes you. It's hard. I know it's hard. It's okay that it's hard. You just have to figure out how to handle the hard part of life and not let it handle you."

"But are you okay?"

"Yes, I'm fine. Just an old woman who has seen enough hard in life to know what you are in for."

Quinn looked up at her. "What do you mean?"

"You need to understand that life is going to come at you fast in the coming months. You must be strong, and you must figure out how to make your own way in the world. Sometimes you gotta take what you need, and sometimes you gotta give what another needs. Sometimes, you get what you need by giving. Life is a game of give and take. Figure that out and you will be on your way to figuring out the how and understanding that the why doesn't matter."

Quinn buried her face in her grandmother's bosom where her tears mixed with the familiar scents of witch hazel and lavender. Her soul found no solace there, as she sobbed uncontrollably in the old woman's loving arms.

CHAPTER 5

"C'mon, let's go!" Sonny bellowed up the stairs. "I have to be there in twenty minutes."

"I'm coming, I'm coming, gimme a minute." Quinn's voice had a sharp edge to it.

"Dammit." Sonny looked at his wife, his dark eyes snapping as he lowered his voice. "I can't be late for this interview. The railroad doesn't hire every day, and I won't get a second chance. Roxanna, get your daughter's ass moving or I am leaving without her and she can walk the two blocks to the church."

"Okay, okay, please be patient. I will go up and hurry her along. Just don't be mad. She's upset enough." Roxanna bustled up the stairs as Sonny stood drumming his fingers on the railing at the bottom of the stairs. Thirty seconds later Roxanna walked down the steps with Quinn in tow.

"Get in the car," Sonny said impatiently, stomping toward the back door, car key in hand.

Roxanna silently stopped Quinn. "Try to relax and just answer the priest's questions. I know you are confused, but this is for your own good, and I know maybe you can't see it now but someday you will understand. I love you. You know that, right? God loves you. Just listen to what Father Schaefer has to say and cooperate with him, okay—?"

The steady blaring of the horn on Sonny's '48 Chevy interrupted Roxanna. Quinn turned and trundled through the house and out the door without saying a word. As she closed the back door to the house, the horn blowing stopped and she looked up to see Sonny's head hanging out the open car window. Words were unnecessary; the expression on his face screamed at Quinn.

Quinn opened the passenger door as a tear rolled down her right cheek. She got into the car and lethargically closed the door. She sat, head down, not saying a word as the silent tears dropped into her lap.

"Aw c'mon, Quinn, stop the cryin'." Sonny's tone softened slightly but insufficiently enough to stop the flow of tears. He backed the car out of the driveway, onto the street, and put it in gear as it sputtered and then accelerated rapidly. "What's the matter with you? This isn't the end of the world. Things will be fine, but you have to get yourself under control."

"I don't want to talk to anyone about this." Quinn's voice was barely audible.

"But your mom thinks this is best, so this is what you have to do. You don't want to hurt your mother, do you? Aren't you a better daughter than to put your mother through more pain?" Sonny looked over at Quinn as he turned into the parking lot of the church. "You have to talk to the priest and make sure nothing you say is going to hurt your family any more than this already has."

Quinn looked at him as the words gut-cut her. She felt the heat of anger boiling up inside her, searing her cheeks.

Oblivious to her pain, Sonny continued, "Do the right thing, Quinn, for your mother's sake. Talk to the priest and tell him what he needs to hear. Then walk home and tell your mother how much you love her. By the time I get home, maybe I'll have some good news about a new job and we can all celebrate with a nice dinner. Okay?" Sonny's voice was now smooth and almost pleading, but his eyes betrayed him. They were dark and demanding. Dangerous, even.

Quinn knew him well. In fact, she probably knew him better than he knew himself. And she always knew how to read those eyes.

"I hope your interview goes well. I will see you at home. I will go talk to this priest, and I will tell my mother I love her. I will do it all." Quinn looked straight ahead for a few brief seconds, then she reached for the door handle, opened the car door, and stepped out. She leaned down and looked defiantly at Sonny with her own dark eyes that no longer shed tears. "Just as I'm supposed to," she added, slamming the car door.

Sonny sat silently and watched her walk up the concrete steps to the double doors of the church. "Little slut," he muttered as he put the car in gear and raced out of the parking lot.

CHAPTER 6

Quinn entered the cool, dark hallway of the church basement. She slowly walked toward the glow of light at the opposite end that shone from Father Schaefer's office. She detested the bizarrely comforting, familiar smell of the church—an odd combination of mustiness, floor wax, old people, candles, and damp books. *It would be good to get some fresh air in here,* she thought.

As she approached the priest's office, she saw him leaning over some papers on his desk, reading intently with his eyeglasses down on his nose. His lips moved as he read. She waited a few seconds, standing in silence, watching this man read to himself. When she could take it no more, she knocked softly on the wooden doorframe. Her irritation with being here was tempered greatly by the intimidation she felt in the presence of the priest. Intimidation fed her irritation. Her stomach ached with anxiety.

"Oh, I didn't hear you come in, Quinn." Father Schaeffer smiled grimly as he stood, gesturing to two chairs in front of his desk. "Sit down." He motioned toward the chair on his right.

"Thank you," Quinn said sweetly as she sat in the chair on the left.

Father Schaeffer sat down behind his mahogany desk and leaned back in his chair. The natural recession of his hairline had neglected the hair in the middle of his head, creating a sparse outcropping of thin, black hair centered perfectly above his large, chalky-white forehead. Quinn thought it looked like an island and found it distracting. His blue eyes didn't seem to be a matched set: his left eye strayed too far to the left, not moving in alignment with the right eye, and his left eyelid drooped a little. This was not the first time she noticed this about him, but it still amused her. She was never sure which eye to look at when speaking to him, so she mostly just alternated her gaze between the one she judged to be the good one and the droopy one.

"Your mother and father were here to see me yesterday."

Quinn concealed her irritation at the priest's mistake. He knew Sonny wasn't her real father.

Father Schaefer stared at Quinn, as if giving her an opportunity to correct him. Quinn looked innocently back at the priest, saying nothing.

"Your parents are concerned about you, as well they should be," he said sternly. "Quinn, this is a serious situation you have gotten yourself into."

"I know."

"What is the fourth commandment?" Father Schaefer's eyebrows arched slightly. Quinn couldn't help but notice the left one didn't arch as high as the right.

"Honor thy father and mother." Quinn's mouth was dry.

"And the sixth?"

"Thou shalt not commit adultery."

"Yes. Or fornication." Father Schaefer paused for Quinn to acknowledge his statement.

Quinn nodded silently and looked away.

"And do you recognize you have broken God's commandments?"

"Yes," Quinn said quietly.

"You are a sinner, Quinn," Father Schaefer said sanctimoniously, passing sentence on her before she saw it coming. He then paused, bowed his head slightly, pressing his fingertips together and resting his lips against his index fingers.

Quinn knew he was carefully choosing the words he was about to say. She concealed her discomfort and waited silently.

"Quinn, you are young and many of life's experiences still await you. But you have experienced some things that shouldn't be experienced until you are much older."

The shame she felt was bubbling to the surface, colliding with her irritation, producing simmering anger inside her. She struggled to maintain her composure and a blank expression. Her mind raced as she searched for the right words.

"Yes, that's true. But sometimes bad things happen, and I don't see why God lets these things happen to someone who isn't a bad person."

"God doesn't let these things happen, Quinn. We make decisions as sinners who fall short of the glory of God and bring these things on ourselves. It saddens God when we disobey him, and these bad things inevitably happen to us because we aren't walking in his light. We are living in Satan's darkness."

"So when bad things happen, even if it isn't our fault, God still holds us accountable and punishes us?" Quinn felt her heart race slightly, her dry tongue trying to stick to the roof of her mouth.

"Quinn, stop!" He looked harshly at her. "If we are honest with ourselves, we know when bad things 'happen,' " he gestured with his fingers in the air to punctuate the quotation marks around the suspect word, "we almost certainly have played some role in those things happening. It's called original sin. It started with Adam and Eve. Do you remember that story?"

"Eve tempted Adam with an apple. Adam ate it, and that was against God's command."

"Yes, that's right. You know right from wrong, and you know the teachings of the church. You must go to confession, acknowledge your sin, and do your penance so God can forgive you."

"Father, that doesn't change my … um … my current situation."

The implication was a transgression Quinn did not intend, and she fumed internally at herself for saying those words. At the same time, she was relieved. Now it was up to him, this leader of the church. What would he do? What *could* he do? She studied the priest's face, looked into his eyes, and peered into his consciousness. She saw a glimmer of recognition in a fleeting instance of naked honesty. For a brief moment, they were on an equal cosmic plane. But then the moment was gone.

The priest looked down and, with his head slightly bowed and his hands clasped before him, began to speak slowly. "Quinn, you must understand that many people find themselves in bad situations. God understands you, your situation, and knows your every thought. You must keep your thoughts clean and pure, and you must not be a temptation for others. Eve had a special power over Adam, and she misused it. Think about that, Quinn. Be pure; be worthy of God's love in your thoughts, in your words, and, most of all, in your actions. Do not exploit another's weakness, for to do so is to be the devil's instrument."

The priest stopped talking and looked at Quinn as she sat motionless, an awkward silence growing between them.

"It seems to be important to your mother that you divulge the name of the baby's father, so he can be held accountable. Are you willing to tell me who this father is?"

"I don't know." Quinn's response was emotionless.

"You don't know who the father is?"

"I don't know." Quinn repeated her response, staring at the front of the priest's desk.

"Your father and I have discussed this at length, and we are both of the opinion that finding the baby's father and holding him accountable matters less than doing the right thing for this child. To bring peace to your family and do right by this child." Father Schaefer stared at Quinn. "You must allow this baby to go to a real family—one with a mother and a father."

"Next week I am going to go live with my Aunt and Uncle in Virginia and have the baby there." Quinn wiped a silent tear from her cheek. "And give it up for adoption there."

"Yes, I know. This is the best thing, for you and the child. I want you to think about what I have said here today and then do the right things so you are pleasing to God. God loves you, and he wants you to be with him in heaven someday. But you must be obedient to him. You have a good family. A good mother and father. You have a good church and are part of the parish family. That is a blessing. You have much to be thankful for, with many people around you to help you walk the right path. You must live each day to be a blessing to those around you and to honor God."

Quinn stood up and nodded slowly, her eyes cast downward. She turned and trudged from Father Schaefer's office, her footslog concealing her anger and defiance.

CHAPTER 7

1954

"It's just an exercise in patience," Aunt Peggy explained to Quinn.

"Mmmm," Quinn replied, as the tip of her tongue wedged itself against the outside corner of her mouth. "Is this chain stitch right?"

"Let's see. Yep, you got it!" Aunt Peggy beamed at her apprentice's work.

Quinn smiled, pleased with herself.

"Now just repeat that stitch for the first row, and you'll be off and running!" Aunt Peggy returned to her chair and resumed working on the dark red afghan, which flowed from her lap to the floor, where it puddled at her feet.

"How do you do it so fast?" Quinn watched her aunt's fingers quickly work the yarn over the hook.

"Well, I've been doing this a long time. It's just a matter of practice and repetition." She looked at Quinn with a serious expression. "Do it long enough and you will be able to crochet without using your tongue."

Quinn giggled along with her aunt. Aunt Peggy was Quinn's favorite of her mom's three sisters. She was always quick to laugh and fun to be around.

Aunt Peggy returned her focus to her crochet needle and yarn, just as a quick movement caught her attention at the window. A robin was banging itself into the window glass.

"Look at that crazy bird, Quinn!"

"What's wrong with him?"

"Oh, he saw his reflection in the glass and thinks it's another bird that has come into his territory," Aunt Peggy replied. "He'll figure it out soon enough or wear himself out in the process. Isn't that just like a man?" She giggled to herself.

"I saved a baby robin at Grandma's house this spring," Quinn said.

"I heard. What happened to it?"

"Well, I put it in a box inside that big evergreen tree, hoping it would learn to fly. Two days later I found the box on the ground, but the bird was gone."

"Well, either the cats got him or he flew out of there," Aunt Peggy said, matter-of-factly.

"I think he learned to fly and he's out there somewhere in the world flying free and happy," Quinn said. "He might even be that bird at the window, you never know!"

"I guess that's true." Aunt Peggy paused. "Say, how do you know it was a boy bird?"

Quinn stopped stitching for a moment. "Gosh, I guess I don't know. I just assumed it was a boy bird. How do you tell the difference in a bird?"

"Well, male birds are always brighter and prettier than female birds," Aunt Peggy said. "But when they are babies, it would be hard to tell."

"Geez, that doesn't seem right," Quinn said. "The boys are pretty, and the girls are ugly?"

"Maybe not ugly, but not as brightly colored as the boys. It's just part of the natural order of things. It's God's way of showing the pecking order in the world, I guess." Aunt Peggy thought for a minute, then grinned. "Heck, Quinn, you know the female birds are smarter than the male birds … you'll never see a female robin banging herself into a window!"

Quinn giggled. "Yes, so maybe God just gave the boy birds the looks because he gave the girl birds the brains!"

Quinn and her Aunt Peggy continued crocheting as the robin continued his battle at the window. Soon he was gone, and the room grew quiet again.

"Do you ever get tired of crocheting, Aunt Peggy?" Quinn broke the silence.

"No, crocheting forces me to be still while my hands can stay busy. It gives me time to think. That's why I like it."

"Doesn't it take a long time to finish something as big as the afghan you're making?

Aunt Peggy smiled. "Yes, it takes a few weeks, depending upon how much time I have to work on it each day."

"But then you give it away. What's the p
work and have nothing to show for it." Qui
aunt.

"That's one perspective, I suppose." Au
never taking her eyes off of her work. "But th
I am making and giving away has value, ye
something else."

"What's that?" Quinn's curiosity was pic

"The process of making something is its real value," Peggy paused and stole a quick glance at Quinn. "The beautiful thing I create, and then give away, creates joy or happiness or gratitude in another person, hopefully."

"So what do you get out of it?"

"Why, the satisfaction of knowing I touched someone's life, even in a small way."

"I see," said Quinn, struggling to understand.

"I don't start a project until I know who I am going to make it for. As I am working on it, I can't help but think about this person, all my memories of them, all of my feelings about them, their strengths and weaknesses as a person—everything."

Aunt Peggy took a breath and looked at Quinn to see if she was still listening. Quinn's big, brown eyes looked back in anticipation.

"Then I also think about what I wish for them in their life and how thankful I am to know them and have them in my life. Some might even call it a prayer, but it goes on a long time in my head."

"Don't you ever run out of things to think about?" Quinn asked.

Aunt Peggy laughed. "Sometimes, but then I just think about their family, and before you know it more ideas come into my head."

"I'll bet you're tired of that person by the time your project is done, huh?"

"Well, no, actually I feel much closer to them and more grateful for them being a part of my life." Aunt Peggy inhaled deeply and exhaled slowly. The room filled with the reliable rhythmic ticking of the wall clock.

"You know, when I think about it, Quinn, I feel like somehow a part of me, my love, gets stitched right into that project and stays with that person."

Quinn contemplated this but said nothing.

"That's the best part of crocheting for me, Q
these things away, why, I'd just end up a crazy,
with a house full of pillows, scarves, and afghans th
any good!"

...ghed at the thought of it, picturing a cartoon version of ...rounded by colorful crocheted projects and yarn sticking out ...dows and doors of her cartoon house.

...unt Peggy put her crochet needle down and looked at Quinn. ...metimes, the best thing we can do for ourselves is to create something ...eautiful and give it away."

CHAPTER 8

The ringing telephone interrupted the chatter and laughter of Roxanna's three small children playing on the floor of the living room.

"Hey," she admonished the children, putting her index finger to her lips. The two boys quieted down, but the middle child, Mary, continued to chat to herself. Roxanna picked up the receiver.

"Hello?"

"Hello, Roxanna." Roxanna immediately recognized the voice of April Pyper from the local Child Welfare Agency. "I'm calling today because there's been some confusion regarding the adoption arrangements."

"Oh?" Roxanna put one hand on her hip as she stood straight up.

"Yes, I received a letter from the Virginia Department of Welfare stating that Mrs. Peggy McColl has signed papers to have the child placed for adoption there in Virginia. We've already selected a family here and all the required paperwork is in place here, as we previously discussed."

"Oh, I see. Well, she must be confused, Miss Pyper," Roxanna said. "I will call her and get this straightened out immediately."

"Very well." April Pyper sounded official in her tone. "Please keep me informed."

"I will call my sister right now and call you back," Roxanna said. "Thank you for calling."

Roxanna cradled the receiver, thought for a moment, and then flipped the pages of her address book until she found the correct entry. She dialed the operator and asked to be connected.

"Hello, McColls," chirped the answer on the other end of the line.

"Peggy, it's Rox." Roxanna, who in the normal course of life had little patience for her younger sister's irritating way of being bright and cheerful, spoke with a slight lilt in her voice.

"Hi, Rox! How are you?"

"I'm fine. Is Quinn close by?"

"No, she and Howard took the little ones to the park for a bit this afternoon," Peggy replied.

Roxanna allowed Peggy to spend the next few minutes in small talk, about kids and the weather and such, out of a sense of strategic obligation.

"Listen, Peggy, I just wanted to check in and see how you and the family are doing, and Quinn, of course, but since this is long distance I probably better get off the line," Roxanna said sweetly.

"Okay, Rox. We're doing fine," Peggy said. "Quinn's doing okay, although she's ready to have this baby. Less than a month away, now."

"Yes ... oh, by the way ... did you get my letter about the adoption process?" Roxanna asked, twirling her hair casually as she waited for her sister's response.

"Why no, I didn't, but it's all taken care of on this end."

"Oh? What do you mean?"

"I signed all the papers with the Virginia agency so it's all done until the baby is born, and then Quinn will have to sign also,"

"Oh, well, I found out that even though the baby is going to be adopted in Virginia," Roxanna chose her words carefully, "the Ohio Child Welfare Agency must handle the paperwork since Quinn's residence is Ohio."

"Oh, my. That seems odd that the Virginia people didn't know?" Peggy squinted her eyes, mentally processing the information.

"Yes, well, it's all a bunch of legal talk that's hard to understand. But everything is handled on this end, so if you can just let them know it's handled, they can deal directly with April Pyper at our local office if they have questions. I'm sure the two agencies can work it out." Roxanna spoke quickly and had to catch her breath.

"Okay then. I will let them know."

Roxanna exhaled, relieved. "Good! This way the Virginia people can go ahead with the adoption process down there, once they speak with April and get the paperwork in order."

"Yes, I suppose that makes sense." Peggy had a hint of uncertainty in her voice. "So does Quinn have to do anything else for the Ohio people?"

"No, not at all. She will just sign the paperwork after the birth, and it will say it's Ohio paperwork, but it's then going to be filed in Virginia for their records. Will you please explain it to Quinn so she's not confused about this?"

"Sure, Rox, I will take care of it. Don't worry about a thing!"

After ending the call with her sister, Roxanna called April Pyper and explained her sister had indeed been confused, thinking the child would be adopted in Virginia and the Virginia authorities would be notified that the Ohio authorities had already handled the adoption. As she placed the receiver on the cradle, she thought again about Peggy's sunny disposition and her ability to always see the good in people.

Roxanna smirked to herself.

CHAPTER 9

Turning his back to his patrons at the bar, Sonny picked up the telephone and dialed. He casually watched the activity in the club reflected in the huge mirror at the back bar as he heard the phone ringing in his ear.

"Father Schaefer," said the voice at the other end.

"It's me. Quinn had the baby today." Sonny didn't need to talk low, as the jukebox music insured his privacy.

"Very well. I will make the call. Everything should be in order for the adoption," the priest replied.

"Okay … listen," Sonny hesitated.

"Yes?"

"I have another matter to discuss with you, but not over the phone. I will come by tomorrow at 2 p.m.," Sonny said.

"Two o'clock. I will be here. See you then."

The phone line clicked once and went silent. Sonny cradled the receiver as he watched a dark silhouette approach the bar from across the room.

"Tom," Sonny recognized his coworker from the railroad yard. "What can I get you?"

"Bell's—neat." Tom pulled his cigarettes from his pocket and placed the pack of Camels on the bar with his zippo lighter neatly aligned on top and sat down.

"This is a first!" Sonny set the drink in front of Tom Mallory. "I've never seen you in here before. Figured you for a Paddy O'Toole's drinker, being the proud Irishman that you are."

Tom chuckled. "I figured I might catch you in here. Heard you were moonlighting."

"Oh, so you came to see me?" Sonny looked at Tom quizzically. "And what do you mean, 'heard I was moonlighting'? You know I've worked here for several years. My family owns the place."

"Yeah, I knew that," Tom leaned in and lowered his voice, causing Sonny to lean forward. "That's not what I meant by moonlighting."

"Huh?" Sonny acted perplexed.

Tom smiled. "I know you've got some action going in the basement. Word is that the cops know about it too."

Sonny's expression never changed. "So who did you hear this from?"

"Can't say," Tom said, "but I've got connections."

"Oh?"

"Listen, in a town this size you can't keep slot machines a secret from the cops. You know that—you've been through it before."

"Yeah, well, people talk about things they know nothing about. You can't believe everything people say, especially about this place," Sonny replied. "And anyway, why do you care?"

"Hummm." Tom took a sip of his drink and set it down. He looked at Sonny and grinned.

"What?" Sonny asked.

Tom said nothing, still grinning, formulating the perfect words to say next.

"Don't just sit there grinning at me," Sonny laughed. He and Tom had always gotten along well at the railroad, but he had never seen this side of the man.

"Let's just say a good businessman knows the value of insurance," Tom said slowly.

"What? You selling insurance now, Tommy?" Sonny played along.

"You could say that." Tom's eyes narrowed slightly as he sipped his drink.

"What kind of policy would you recommend?" Sonny asked. "I mean, considering my risk profile as you understand it."

"You need something that would give you an opportunity to eliminate your risk at the local level. I can make it happen."

"I see," Sonny said. "And assuming I was interested in purchasing this policy, it seems fairly limited. What about higher level risk?"

"We know ahead of time when a particular risk is going to occur. We can make sure you know also, so you can plan accordingly." Tom removed a Camel from its pack and lit it, clicking the zippo closed. His nostrils moved slightly inward as he sucked on the cigarette and inhaled and then flared out as he exhaled the smoke from his lungs. He looked at Sonny and arched his eyebrows.

Sonny, leaning on the bar, studied Tom's face. He flashed a grin. "If I decide I need insurance, you'll be the guy I call," Sonny said.

Tom dropped two one-dollar bills on the bar and stood to leave. "I've gotta get out of here. Too much Italian in here for me," he said with a wink.

"Okay, you dumb mick." Sonny smiled. "We'll be talking."

Sonny placed the glass in the sink and wiped down Tom's spot at the bar, contemplating his visit. A voice interrupted his thoughts.

"Sonny—one more," a gravelly voice grumbled from the end of the bar.

"Coming up, Sal." Sonny drew a mug of beer from the tap, overfilling it and causing it to slosh out as he set it down in front of his cousin.

"Hey, careful! You're wasting good beer." Sal smiled sloppily. He leaned in, motioning with his head for Sonny to move closer. "Who was that fella who was just in here?"

"Tom Mallory. I work with him at the railroad."

"Tom Mallory, Tom Mallory ... yeah, now I remember him!" Sal exclaimed, eyes brightening.

Sonny looked surprised. "From where?"

"I met him over at Serge and Edie's a few months back. He and Serge were talking about Tom's brother who's a priest in charge of an orphanage in Ireland."

"Oh?"

"Yeah, turns out Tom helped Serge and Edie with the adoption of their baby, which came from the orphanage Tom's brother runs."

"Oh yeah?" Sonny wiped off the bar. "I knew they adopted a baby, but I never knew where it came from." Sonny's mind was racing. Serge, a local police officer, was married to Sonny's cousin, Edie. Sonny and Serge always got along okay, and Sonny always trusted him. Serge had a reputation as a good cop and had recently been promoted to sergeant.

Sonny's brain was spinning. He looked around the room and then back at Sal. He leaned in, speaking quietly, "You ever heard anything about Serge being dirty?"

"Nah," Sal said, "not really. I mean you hear things all the time, and I know there's dirty cops in this town, but I've never heard Serge's name specifically. But, you never know."

Sal finished his beer and looked at Sonny, blinking with more energy than necessary. Sonny knew this was Sal's hypervigilant, sober state. He loved the guy, but he had become quite an odd creature since he came home from the war, shell-shocked. He drank too much but had an uncanny ability to keep his ear to the ground. People confided in Sal, probably because they dismissed him as a drunk or just plain stupid. A drunk, he was. But stupid? Never. He engendered good will from those around him, as he was as likeable as he was quirky. Whenever he talked about something he thought was important, he blinked like he was trying to clear blurred vision. Over and over again.

"What?" Sonny asked, distracted with his thoughts.

"All this talkin' is makin' me thirsty," Sal said. His enunciation was sloppy as the words sloshed in this mouth like water in a bucket. "Absolutely parched. One of those on-the-house beers quenches a guy's thirst." He blinked at Sonny, like Morse code, his facial expression earnestly telegraphing the seriousness of the moment.

Sonny smirked and pulled the tap to refill Sal's mug. He set it down in front of Sal, about three-fourths full.

"Hey! You only gave me a half a beer," Sal said indignantly.

"On-the-house beer," Sonny replied without hesitation. "It's like espresso, comes in smaller sizes. Plus, you bitched so much about me spilling the last one. I didn't want to see you upset again." He chuckled at his own joke.

"I'm disappointed in you, Sonny," Sal said as he brought the mug to his lips and took several gulps of the beer. Sonny grabbed the mug, topped it off, and set it back in front of Sal.

"Now, after this one you're a paying customer again."

Sal smiled. "You are a fine proprietor of this upstanding establishment."

CHAPTER 10

Sonny sat in the only cushioned chair in the room, an overstuffed leather armchair that looked out of place in the sparse office. It sat, alone, in the far corner of the office next to a floor lamp and a bookshelf. Father Schaefer settled in behind his desk and looked at Sonny.

"I want to make another donation," Sonny said, without emotion.

"Oh?" The priest's facial expression registered a look of surprise.

"Yes, for the Orphan and Widows Fund, same amount as before."

"Another baby? And what arrangements must be made for this donation?" Father Schaefer asked, unable to conceal his irritation.

"Same as with Quinn," Sonny replied, nearly cutting off the priest. "I have a sister in need. I will get details to you later."

"Sister?" Schaefer was incredulous. "Your own sister?"

Sonny's dark eyes locked on the priest momentarily. Words were unnecessary.

"Is this the sister in Buffalo?"

Sonny nodded.

"I see." Schaefer hesitated and eyed Sonny carefully. "It seems this could become a pattern."

"Two donations is hardly a pattern," Sonny said, irritated with the priest's attitude. He bit the side of his thumb, gnawing the annoying little hard fleck of skin beside his right thumbnail.

"Yes, well, I suppose that's true, but two so close together could raise a few eyebrows."

"Well, that's your problem. Figure it out. You're a smart guy. You'll come up with something. Just keep it respectable," Sonny said, not looking at the priest.

The priest and Sonny sat quietly for a moment, Sonny still chewing on this thumb, while the priest digested his current dilemma. The tension in the air was nothing of concern for either man and certainly nothing new. They had known each other for twenty years, since Sonny was a child and Schaefer was a new priest. The road they had travelled together was rocky but familiar, and neither had any intention of changing course. Their destinies were intertwined, yet for all this history, they neither loved nor hated one another.

Schaefer broke the silence. "Perhaps the donations should be smaller."

Sonny grinned. "Sure," he said coyly, already knowing what the priest was about to say.

The priest gave him an exasperated look. "You know what I mean," he said as he leaned forward in his chair slightly. "Same amount, but make three or four smaller donations over a period of time."

Sonny contemplated the suggestion. He liked to make a big splash with his money.

"That makes sense," Sonny said, pausing to bite his thumb again. "I'll just make four donations, one every two months. I'll make the first one in a month, and the last one will be one month after the baby's born."

Schaefer nodded slowly. The silence resumed, and neither man showed any signs of movement. It was as if they needed unspoken time together to process their individual strategies and reset their mutual interests. A distant door was closed noisily, a sign one of the Sisters of the Sacred Hearts of Jesus and Mary was moving about the building.

"Your family is lucky to have a guy like you to help them with their problems," Schaefer said, baiting Sonny.

"I suppose," Sonny said, pretending not to know what the priest was implying. "I just try to make sure things are taken care of."

"Have you thought about what would happen if things couldn't be taken care of?"

"What?"

"I'm just saying, don't make the mistake of believing you can fix every problem."

"I haven't found one yet that I can't fix," Sonny retorted.

"Yes, I know," Schaefer replied. "That's the problem."

"What?" Sonny leaned forward, eyebrows raised, irritation in his voice. "You are making no sense."

"Over-confidence can be a weakness," Schaefer paused to let the words sink in and raised his hands as Sonny started to speak. "Look, you need to think about the long-term, big picture, not just live for today. So far you have been able to do damage control quite well. But in the right circumstances, you can lose control. And losing control means exposure. Neither of us can afford that."

"Yeah, okay," Sonny sat back in his seat, the sarcasm evident in his voice. "Don't act like you are all high and mighty because you're wearing that collar. You need me, and you can't do what I can do."

"You're right. It's a good arrangement we have. But it's only good as long as we both maintain it, and sometimes that means putting off what we want today, small picture, for what we can have tomorrow, big picture."

Sonny went back to work on his thumb. The room was silent for a few seconds as the priest's words slowly drained into his brain, penetrating his stubbornness.

"We have been presented with an opportunity," Schaefer said finally.

Sonny looked up, surprised. "What's that?"

"I understand you know Tom Mallory?"

Sonny sat forward in his chair, unable to conceal his interest. "Yeah, I know Tom." He was certain it was more than mere coincidence that he had just spoken to Tom yesterday, making arrangements for his "insurance policy."

"He has a proposition for us."

"What's that?"

"Relax, Sonny," Schaefer chided him, toying with him for a few seconds longer. "We have an opportunity to serve our Catholic families in a unique way, specifically those couples who are unable to conceive children."

Sonny's mind immediately went to Sal's comment about Mallory's brother in Ireland. "I'm listening," he said.

"There is a shortage of healthy white babies in America available for adoption. There are unwed mothers in Ireland. Most of them destitute and without the resources to properly raise a child. We have an opportunity to bring those babies here and place them in good homes."

"So isn't the church already doing that?"

"In a limited fashion, yes. The key word being *limited.* There are immigration quotas that limit the number of babies the church can bring in."

"So why does Mallory need us?"

"For two reasons. First, your connections at the Buffalo border entry in upstate New York. Your job would be to get the babies into the United States from Canada. You know how to do that, and I don't need to know the details."

"And the second reason?"

"Once the babies are here, they will be legally adopted through a nonprofit adoption agency associated with the Catholic church."

"Catholic Charities?" Sonny asked.

"No, a local agency, Stork Ministries, a nonprofit organization we are forming."

"Nonprofit? Why would we do this for free?"

"We're not. Nonprofit just means we have certain tax-exempt privileges. We can make money; we just can't show a profit."

"Wouldn't it be better to do this away from public view? A nonprofit? Aren't we just asking for trouble?"

"A nonprofit, publicly visible, Catholic adoption agency lends a certain respectability to the process, don't you think?"

"So where does the money come from?" Sonny was intrigued.

"The Diocese in Belfast pays all expenses for childbirth and the care and housing of the mother. They also provide a small stipend for the baby, to defray travel expenses." Father Schaefer was being methodical in his explanation.

"Okay, but I am not hearing any payday yet."

"The couple adopting the child—that's a substantial source of income," Father Schaefer explained. "You see, we are making these babies available to wealthy Catholic families, willing to pay substantial sums for the joy a child will bring into their homes. That's part of my job in all this. "

"So how are you going to find wealthy couples who want an Irish baby?" Sonny challenged the priest.

"Irish baby? These babies are white babies—that's all they care about and all they need to know. Of course, as a responsible religious organization concerned for the welfare of all parties, we hold as confidential all information regarding the birthmother. Those records will never be accessible to the adoptive parents or the child."

"What about people who cannot pay top dollar?"

Father Schaefer looked at him, brow furled. He spoke as if he were stating the obvious: "Why, Sonny, God provides for rich and poor alike. They just go on a waiting list at Catholic Charities, as usual."

CHAPTER 11

"Get your ass out of that car, you little bitch!" Roxanna grabbed a handful of flowing auburn hair and pulled Karen Clemens from the front seat of the Chevy.

"Stop it! I didn't do nothing, Roxanna!" Karen pleaded.

Roxanna slapped the girl's cheek twice and began kicking at her, cursing, and screaming. Karen whimpered and cried, like an abused kitten.

"Hey, knock it off!" Sonny yelled, hustling around to the passenger side of the car to calm Roxanna down. The shoppers in the public square stopped and gawked. After all, it wasn't every Saturday afternoon you got to see this kind of action downtown. Mothers were appalled and tried to cover their children's ears, while fathers couldn't help but laugh at the tawdry spectacle as they enjoyed Roxanna's vivacious curves accented by her navy blue capri slacks.

"Don't tell me to knock it off!" Roxanna screamed at Sonny. "What's this little slut doing in your car?"

A collective gasp escaped from the crowd, followed by the pious buzz of murmurs.

"Roxanna," Sonny kept his voice low as he surveyed the gathering crowd. He held both of her wrists in his hands as she attempted to pull away. "Stop it now and get in the car." His dark eyes were menacing, and Roxanna, who was now crying, at least stopped talking. Karen was huddled against the rear fender of the car parked in front of the candy store Sweet Treats. It seemed every local resident had chosen today to shop, as the sidewalks were jammed with people.

"What's the problem, here?" A voice boomed behind Sonny. He

turned to see a blue uniform parting the crowd, a local police officer he didn't know.

"Just a little family matter, Officer." Sonny looked at the officer for a response, still holding Roxanna's wrists.

"Who's this?" the officer asked Sonny.

"My wife," Sonny said, flatly, looking at Roxanna.

"Who's the girl?" the officer pointed with his nightstick to Karen.

"She's a whore!" Roxanna offered. Sonny squeezed her wrists tighter and looked at the officer, rolling his eyes momentarily.

"Get your wife under control," the officer instructed as a police cruiser stopped in the street, double-parked next to Sonny's car. Sonny saw Serge DiPetro hop out of the car.

"Hey Serge," Sonny said, resignation in his voice as the first officer looked at the sergeant and then back at Sonny. "Little family problem is all."

"Okay," Serge said quietly, "let's everyone calm down." Serge instructed the other officer to take Karen to his cruiser, place her in the back seat, and record her information for the report.

"Let me go, Sonny," Roxanna quietly sobbed. The fight was out of her, at least for now.

"Let her go, Sonny," Serge said quietly, then looked at Roxanna. "You, sit in the car and don't say anything, understand?"

"Yes," she whimpered. Sonny released his grip on her wrists, and Roxanna compliantly opened the passenger door and climbed into the front passenger seat of Sonny's car, slamming the door behind her.

"What the hell, Sonny? In the Public Square on a Saturday afternoon?" Serge chuckled surreptitiously, lips barely moving, lest the thinning crowd of onlookers think he was performing his duties inappropriately.

"Yeah, well, I didn't pick the place, Serge." Sonny looked down, trying to act nonchalant.

"How old is she?" Serge nodded toward his cruiser, unable to suppress a grin.

"Old enough." Sonny kept a straight face.

"A little advice ... keep her out of the Public Square, maybe?"

"Yeah, probably a good idea." Sonny shifted his weight slightly and put his hands in his pants pockets. He saw Roxanna sitting in the car, staring straight ahead as if mesmerized by something nobody else could see.

Serge lifted his blue police cap, the gold shield glimmering in the afternoon sun, and ran his fingers through his hair. He replaced the cap on his head, adjusting it for a perfect level fit, unlike the other older officer whose hat was cocked at an odd angle from side to side. He removed his pocket notepad from his inner jacket pocket and, with pen in hand, flipped the pad open.

"Aw, what're you doing, Serge? You writing me? For what?" Sonny kept his voice low and his face expressionless.

"No, I am not writing you," Serge said quietly, looking up from his notepad. "But these fine citizens here expect to see some kind of justice done, you know. They want to see their tax dollars spent wisely."

"Okay." Sonny caught on.

"So," Serge continued, looking down at his pad as he continued to write earnestly, "I am going to give them their money's worth while we stand here. Once Officer Graham there finishes getting information from the girl, we'll both be on our way. I'll take the girl home, and you get to deal with Roxanna. Now, I have a question for you."

"What's that?"

"Ever read Ralph Waldo Emerson?"

"Who? Is he a reporter?"

Serge, knowing Sonny was lost in all of this, looked up for a moment, flipped to the next page of his notebook, and quickly made a short entry. He then ripped the page out and handed it to Sonny with a stern look.

"Take care, Sonny. Consider this closed." Serge turned on his heel and walked to his cruiser as the foot patrolman closed Karen in the back seat of the car.

Sonny glanced at the paper Serge had handed him.

Good men must not obey the laws too well.

Sonny climbed behind the wheel of his car and started the engine. Roxanna sat silently, braced for what was coming.

"What the hell is wrong with you?" Sonny screamed as he accelerated toward home. "Why are you acting so crazy?"

"Sonny," Roxanna cried softly, tears slowly sliding down her face, "I know you been sleeping with her."

"What? No, Rox," Sonny lied. "Why would you think that? I was just giving her a ride!"

"I see how she looks at you, and I know. I'm not stupid."

"What do you know? Nothing!" Sonny beat his fist on the dashboard of the car. "Nothing! She's the babysitter, dammit!"

Roxanna said nothing as she stared at the passing buildings.

"I can't help it if women are attracted to me. It's just part of who I am; it's not anything I say or do. I'm just being me." Sonny glanced over at Roxanna, gauging her reaction but seeing none. "She's probably got a crush on me, that's all. She's a crazy teenager. She's too young for me anyway. I have you, Roxanna, what would I want with her?"

Roxanna looked cautiously at Sonny. She sat silently for a few minutes.

"Really? Do you mean that, Sonny?"

"Yes, of course. Have I ever done anything to make you think I don't love you? Have I ever had an affair? Don't I bring home money for you and our three kids? And Quinn? What do you want from me, Rox?"

"I'm sorry, Sonny, I guess sometimes I think maybe you want someone younger. I love you and want to take care of you, and I don't want to share you with anyone else."

Sonny looked over at Roxanna and sighed. He put his hand on her thigh. "You don't have to. But you can never pull that crap again like you just did, understand?"

She nodded and wiped her face with her hand. "I'm sorry."

Sonny smiled and touched her face with the back of his hand. "Don't make me lose my temper like that ever again." His dark eyes were intense, and although his voice was calm and soothing, his eyes belied the turbulence he could unleash spontaneously.

Roxanne knew she would have to work harder at being a better person, more deserving of a man like Sonny, or she would lose him.

CHAPTER 12

1955

"You need to go to confession for your sins," Sonny's voice was quiet but commanded the darkness.

There was no reply.

"Quinn?" Irritation cloaked the word. "Did you hear me?"

"I heard." Quinn muttered. She didn't have the energy for a fight, and she knew she could never win anyway, although she fantasized about killing him.

Sonny said nothing and left the room, leaving Quinn alone in the darkness with her demons.

* * *

The deep red object laying in the sun-drenched, emerald-green backyard was moving. Quinn approached it, curious what it could be. As she drew near, she realized it was an afghan with a baby curled up inside. Quinn bent to look at the baby and saw its coal black hair, bushy hair for a baby, and lots of it, so thick and coarse it stuck straight out in tufts, in all directions. Something was flapping under the afghan. She dropped to her knees, pulled back the afghan, and saw one of the baby's big, black wings flapping, but the other one was still. She touched the broken wing gently. The baby, wearing only a bright white diaper, looked at her with coal black eyes. The baby stopped moving and smiled. Then the smile faded as the baby furled its brow and cocked its head to one side. Quinn didn't know babies could do that. She waited for the baby to ask the question, but he said nothing. The broken wing started slowly oozing a thick, red substance, right in the middle where the two wing bones formed a joint. It reminded Quinn of a kite frame, like she made with sticks and newspapers. *It's baby bird blood*, Quinn thought. Her mind raced. What should she do? She knew she mustn't leave the baby in the yard, exposed to the neighborhood cats, but she couldn't pick the baby up or it would die because of her touch. She looked up at her grandma standing there before her.

"If I get the baby into a box before he gets here, we can hide him in the tree, Grandma!" Quinn exclaimed.

Her grandmother, standing perfectly still, her eyes never leaving Quinn's face, said nothing.

"Hurry, help me!"

"No, Quinn," Grandma said in a deep voice. "It's not a boy; it's a girl. See the black wings?"

"Oh." Quinn rocked back, sitting with her knees tucked under her, rocking back and forth slightly. "I didn't know."

"Are you at this again, Quinn?" Roxanna asked derisively. "This thing isn't going to survive. That's why it's out here alone."

"But, Mom, it's a baby that needs help, that's all," Quinn protested. "Once it learns to walk, it will lose its wings." All she wanted to do was put the baby in the tree, where it would be safe.

"It's nature's way, Quinn." Roxanna lit a cigarette and took a drag on it as she stood between Sonny and Grandma.

"Let me put it in the tree, and then I will forget all about it. Please?" Quinn looked pleadingly at her mother, who was shaking her head. Grandma said nothing.

"I have to cut the tree down today, Quinn." Sonny showed her a large saw with sharp teeth, the kind two men normally push and pull. But she knew Sonny could use it all by himself. "I know how to handle these things, Quinn. I understand nature."

"Come on, Quinn, let's go inside," Grandma said quietly. "Let nature take its course. Maybe the baby will fly on its own before the tree comes down."

Roxanna took another drag and stared at Quinn.

As she and Grandma walked to the house, Sonny called after her, "It's okay, Quinn. I know how to make this all work out. God helps those who help themselves."

Quinn cried for the bird baby with the black wings as Grandma soaked up her tears with the tail of the tablecloth in the little kitchen.

* * *

Quinn woke up crying and sat up straight in her bed. It took a moment to clear her head. She wanted to go back into the nightmare to fix everything she could fix and to see her dead grandma. Oh, how she missed Grandma. It was comforting to talk to her again, even if the dream made her cry. She was relieved it was only a nightmare but sad it was only a dream. She sat, staring at the floral print on the blanket, seeing only her memories. The fog of sleep lifted, and a kaleidoscope of emotion washed over her as the surreal stillness of the night collided with the impending demands of a cold, new day.

Suddenly she was blindsided with the triple gut-punch of loss in an unfamiliar and brutal way. She sobbed, her petite frame heaving and convulsing with the uncontrollable flow of raw tears that rose up angrily as her mind was haunted with painful memories of Grandma, of her lost child, of even her lost baby robin. She was alone in her grief, unable to make sense of her life, yet unwilling to let the go of the past. Those scarce and pathetic memories were all that was left, and the pain was the price to be paid for her refusal to let go. Anger, fused with desperation and hopelessness, surged within her. Her cheeks were hot as the tears burned their way down her face. Emptiness consumed her, except for the part of her she reserved for her hatred of Sonny. Where the emptiness had not yet found its way into her being, anger had.

"Why did you leave me when I needed you most?" she asked in desperation. The empty room stood silent.

CHAPTER 13

"It's the most pain I've ever felt. Until the gas starts working, but that doesn't help much."

Bonnie Murphy's eyes were wide as she listened intently to her best friend's description of childbirth.

"What kind of pain?" Bonnie asked, as she puffed awkwardly on her cigarette. "Where does it hurt, like inside you?"

"Yes, all through your box and everywhere," Quinn said. "What do you think? It's a big baby coming out of that tiny space."

Bonnie giggled, but Quinn was annoyed. She didn't mean to be funny.

"Let's talk about something else," Quinn snapped.

Bonnie looked at Quinn, puzzled, but said nothing as they continued walking, each with school books under one arm and a cigarette in their free hands. The cold air bit at their bare legs, exposed below their skirts. Bonnie had grown accustomed to Quinn's moodiness, even if she didn't always understand it. The girls had struck up an immediate friendship when they both got caught smoking at school on the same day and served detention together. Bonnie enjoyed Quinn's sense of humor, and Quinn found Bonnie to be a person who accepted her for who she was, without judgment. She told Bonnie things she could tell no one else.

A loud blast from a beat-up, blue Chevy startled Quinn, who was deep in thought, causing her to flinch. Bonnie started laughing as the car puttered on by, the teenage boy craning his neck in the girls' direction.

"You know who that was?" Bonnie asked, not so much as a question but as an introduction to an impending, exciting pronouncement.

"No, but I wish he had that horn up his ass."

Bonnie laughed aloud and looked over at her friend. "Did you pee just a wee, Quinn?"

Quinn grudgingly laughed, unable to help herself. "No!" she replied and then laughed a little more, looking at Bonnie. "I almost did piss my pants." Both girls guffawed for a moment.

"So, anyway ... who was that?"

"That, my friend Quinn," Bonnie paused for dramatic effect, "is Charlie Freund." Bonnie looked at Quinn with eyebrows raised.

"Okay, so what? Why're you looking at me like that?"

"I happen to know Charlie Freund wants to be *your* friend." Bonnie watched Quinn's face for a reaction.

"Who says?" Quinn was skeptical. "How do you know?"

"He asked my older brother about you because he knows you and I are friends. He told my brother he thinks you're cute."

Quinn didn't react at first, caught by surprise. The girls continued walking, and soon the Chevy passed them going the opposite direction. The boy driver waved and smiled, and Bonnie returned the waved. Quinn looked directly into Charlie Freund's eyes and couldn't help but smile.

"See, I told you!" Bonnie said as soon as the car had passed by.

Quinn's smile faded.

"Does he know?"

"Know what?" Bonnie asked, and then a look of recognition crossed her face. "Oh, that. Yes, I'm sure he does. Everyone talks, you know."

"What do you think they are saying about me?" Quinn's voice was soft, causing Bonnie to turn and look her friend in the eye.

"Who cares what they are saying?" Bonnie fired back. "But honestly I don't know what anyone says or thinks about you because they know better than to say anything bad to me."

Quinn smiled, but her concerns were evident in her troubled expression.

"It wasn't easy to come back here," she said heavily. "It's not like I had a choice, but I knew when I came back I would be the outcast."

"Do you feel like that now?" Bonnie's tone was sympathetic.

"There are some people who treat me different. Girls who act stuck-up all of a sudden. But then, some of the boys are a lot friendlier. Just because they want something."

"Well, I say anybody who has a problem with you can go fly a kite! Some of those girls just haven't gotten caught, that's all. They act like they are pure as the driven snow, but I doubt it. Quinn, ignore those snobs. You get to start over with a clean slate, all that other stuff is behind you, and you can forget it."

"I wish it were that easy, Bonnie. But it's not."

"Why not?"

"Well, because, it's just not," Quinn snapped. "I can't just forget everything."

"I don't see why not. It's over. You deserve to move on." Bonnie squeezed Quinn's shoulder.

"You don't understand."

"I understand enough to know that you can't change what has happened, so you have to just keep living your life. So live it."

"But it isn't just my life that's affected here" Quinn's voice caught. "Somewhere out there is a baby, my baby, that I let them take away from me. I can't forget that."

Bonnie was silent, not sure what to say to her friend. She thought for a few minutes as their footsteps took them closer to their homes, which were only one street apart.

"Did you want to keep your baby?" Bonnie asked. "I mean, I thought you wanted to give it up to a good home."

"I don't know; it was confusing. I wasn't given a choice, but I feel like I did the wrong thing. I am that baby's mother, and now she is out there without me. I can't stop thinking about her." A tear slipped down Quinn's cheek; she wiped it away with the sleeve of her coat.

"I'm sure she's in a good home, with a mom and dad, and she'll be fine," Bonnie said in the most soothing voice she could muster.

"I know," Quinn said, through more tears. "I know it's probably best for her to be with a real family, but I worry about her and wish I could see her again, hold her in my arms. I feel like I did something wrong that I can never undo."

"You can't undo it, Quinn. You just can't," Bonnie said. "You have no ability to change it, no control over any of it."

"I know. But I'm so sad about it all." Quinn paused, collecting her thoughts before continuing. "You asked me about how it felt to have a baby—the pain and everything."

"Yeah?"

"Well, the pain is bad. But when the baby comes out, it's so magical to hear her cry the first time and to know you created this little life. She's a part of you, but now a whole new life in her own right. Once you've done that, you know the pain was worth it and you would do it all over again just to experience the new life before you."

"I can't imagine it, Quinn."

"No, you can't, Bonnie, you can't imagine it. You have to experience it. Now I understand why they call it the miracle of childbirth. Something so painful can be so beautiful. It's like magic. More than magic." Quinn looked away as the tears welled up in her eyes again. They stopped walking. Bonnie leaned against a tree, waiting for Quinn to say more.

Quinn inhaled and squared her shoulders. "Then they take something beautiful, and they steal it from you, right there as you watch them do it, even help them do it. So after all the pain, you produce a beautiful, new, little life, and all you are left with is a big hole inside you where that baby used to be." Quinn's tears flowed freely, and she felt a sense of relief as the words, which in some ways surprised her, flowed out of her.

"Quinn," Bonnie said quietly, "maybe you should talk to someone about this?"

"Who? Why?" Quinn couldn't hide the sharp edge to her voice. "Nobody cares, except you."

"What about talking to the priest? Maybe he can help you?"

"Priest? Ha!" Quinn sniffed in disgust. "He already told me I was going to hell for this."

"He said that?" Bonnie's eyes widened.

"Not exactly, but that's what he meant," Quinn replied, running her sleeve across her face again. "Know what I think? I think giving away my baby created a hole in my soul, and there is no room in heaven for a soul that isn't whole."

CHAPTER 14

"Maybe a little more rouge to highlight your cheeks," Roxanna suggested, standing behind Quinn and looking at her daughter in the mirror.

"This feels weird."

"It looks good, Quinn," Roxanna replied. "Get used to it. Men like their women to look good."

Quinn finished applying the rouge and looked at her mother as Roxanna fussed over the final touches to Quinn's hair styling. Her dark hair framed her face perfectly as it shone in its fullness, just reaching her shoulders from the part in the middle of her head.

"Yes, that's better. Now go get dressed. You've only got one hour before you have to be there." Roxanna was remarkably calm tonight and even supportive; she even loaned Quinn a necklace and earrings, a formal gown, and shoes for her junior prom.

Quinn slipped on the emerald-green, floor-length gown with the boat neckline. The sleeveless chiffon dress flowed from its natural three-inch waistline in two-inch pleats, forming an A-line silhouette. Quinn fastened the three-strand, choker-style necklace, each strand containing two one-quarter-inch, white, faux pearls alternating with two like-sized, green, glass crystals for the length of the necklace. She liked how the emerald-green dress perfectly matched the glass crystals in the necklace and the earrings.

"You look like a younger version of me," Roxanna boasted as she stood in the doorway. "Oh, I've had some good times in that gown." Roxanna always dressed to the nines, especially when she was working at the club or when out socializing. Quinn never felt she had her mother's sense of style, although ever since she was small, so small her memories were cloudy, Quinn loved to sneak a peek into Roxanna's ample jewelry box and ogle the many shiny, colorful pieces neatly arranged there. It was a wonderfully enchanted place, and as a young child Quinn was certain even princesses didn't have as much jewelry as her mother.

"Hurry up, Quinn," Roxanna said as she turned to descend the stairway. "You don't want to be late to your first prom."

Alone in the room, Quinn slipped on her mother's black dress shoes, the ones with the fashionable two-inch heel, and liked how she immediately gained some much needed height to her five-foot, petite frame. Slipping on the white gloves, she studied the woman in the mirror before her. She never realized how much makeup, hairstyling, and formal clothing could change a person's appearance. Turning from side to side, she studied herself from all angles and liked what she saw. She even tried to view her backside, but almost lost her footing thanks to the heels. She practiced extending her gloved hand as she accepted an invitation to dance from a phantom gentleman. What is the proper way to hold your hand out? How do you do this without looking silly? Quinn tried several more times, unsatisfied that she had perfected the technique.

As the beautiful, young lady stood before the mirror, donned in a borrowed dress, jewelry, and shoes, wearing them all with stunning poise and grace, doubt seeped in. She stood there, flawless, searching for imperfections. Soon she found what nobody else could ever find. She knew the truth, even if nobody else recognized it. This wasn't the real Quinn, and no amount of borrowed clothing or jewelry or painted-on makeup could change that, nor could it mask the real Quinn for long.

She took one last look in the mirror, even as she knew from the sinking feeling in the pit of her stomach that she was masquerading as someone she could never be. The excitement drained from her, excitement she told herself she felt because that is what teenagers going to prom are supposed to feel, but her secret, among many, was she didn't feel that excitement, at least not in the way she was certain she should have felt it. What she felt was dread that someone would see her foolishness in attempting to make herself into something she wasn't, something she had no right to be. *Nothing about this whole prom thing ever felt right*, Quinn thought. *What am I doing?*

She continued studying her reflection and knew this costume wouldn't work. It seemed too much like a teenage version of Halloween, but without the candy and the fun. Quinn was too old for childish Halloween dress-up and not good enough for teenage Halloween.

Quinn was embarrassed by what she saw in the mirror because she knew the image wasn't real. She slowly began removing the jewelry, the shoes, and then the dress. As she went into the bathroom to wash off her mask, she felt a weight lifting off of her shoulders—relief she didn't have to face anyone at prom tonight. Yet, she felt a sense of disappointment in her realization that she would never fit in.

Quinn slipped on her own clothes and went downstairs and headed for the front door, trying to leave unnoticed. Her mother called after her. "Quinn, are you—" Roxanna stopped mid-sentence, surprised by her daughter's sudden appearance in capri slacks and a plain, white blouse.

"I'm not going," Quinn said curtly. "It's stupid."

"What? Why not?" Roxanna prodded. "I thought you wanted to go! Why did we do your hair and makeup?"

"I don't want to talk about it," Quinn said. "It's stupid, and I'm not going."

"I wish you would have decided before I spent all afternoon getting you ready," Roxanna said.

"I feel stupid wearing all that stuff. I don't fit in."

"You don't fit it because you don't try to fit in, Quinn."

"What does that mean?" Quinn asked, surprised at her mother's remark.

"Sometimes you have to go along to get along. And if you do that enough, eventually people will accept you." Roxanna studied Quinn's face. "If you don't go to prom, people will talk because you didn't go. All the good kids are going, and so should you."

"They don't want me there," Quinn protested. "And if they do want me there, it's just so they have someone to talk about."

"Now, you know that's not true," Roxanna said firmly. "You have friends you can hang around with, and I am sure some boy will ask you to dance."

"I doubt that."

"Do what you want to do, but I say you need to get dolled up and go try to make friends with these kids you think don't like you. If you show them you are normal—try to be like them, Quinn, see it their way—they will come around." Roxanna sighed. "But do whatever you want, I can't force you to go."

"I can't be like them, Mom. It's too late for that," Quinn said, the regret heavy in her voice. "I'll be back later." She turned and walked out the front door.

Roxanna stood for a moment watching Quinn walk down the front sidewalk, then muttered to herself, "You've always been a strange child. I did my best, but you refuse to see the world as it is. I don't know where you went wrong."

CHAPTER 15

"So was he nervous?"

"No, not really. At least he didn't act like it."

"I can't believe you and Charlie have been going steady for a month and he still hadn't met your parents," Bonnie said. "My mom and dad wouldn't have let me out of the house for the first date without meeting the boy."

"They didn't know anything about it, I made sure of that." Quinn looked at Bonnie, who was sitting on the concrete stoop outside the back door of her house. The late afternoon sun shone bright. This was the first hot day of June, with the temperature hovering near 80 degrees.

"How did you keep it from them?" Bonnie asked.

"It's not hard. After all, it's not like they care what I am doing as long as I don't make any trouble for them."

"So what did Sonny say to Charlie?" Bonnie wanted the details.

"He asked him where he worked, what his plans were for his life, if he'd ever been in trouble. Mostly stuff like that."

"Did he tell Charlie he better treat you right? Give him the third degree?"

"No, not really." Quinn thought for a minute. "No, neither Mom nor Sonny said anything like that. They just wanted to know more about him, I guess."

"What did Charlie say afterward?" Bonnie continued her line of questioning. Quinn indulged her for lack of anything better to talk about today.

"Not much. I think he was relieved Sonny seemed to like him. He knew of Sonny before he met me, but he had never met him."

"How did he know about Sonny?" Bonnie asked.

Quinn looked at Bonnie, her eyebrows raised slightly.

"Oh. Of course." The realization hit her. "Does it bother you that Charlie gets mixed up in that kind of thing?"

"Yes and no," Quinn answered. "Yes, because I don't want him to get arrested. But no, because I don't think he's hurting anyone."

Bonnie considered Quinn's reasoning but couldn't leave it alone. "But he is stealing, Quinn."

"Yeah, but it's only from a business. It's not like he's stealing from a person. I mean, I don't think it's right, but at the same time, insurance covers it for a business. He's not going in someone's house or anything. Nobody is getting hurt." Quinn looked at Bonnie, seeking some validation of her rationalization.

"Yeah, I suppose that's true." The uncertainty was evident in Bonnie's voice.

"I love him, Bonnie. I will stand by him, because he makes me feel like nobody has ever made me feel before." Quinn smiled, causing Bonnie to snicker.

"Look at you, all lovey-dovey in love!" Bonnie teased. "That boy swept you off your feet, didn't he?"

Quinn's smile broke into a grin. "Yes, I guess so. I just think he's strong and funny and dreamy. I love him, and he loves me."

"So," Bonnie couldn't resist the temptation, "have you, uh ... you know?" She gestured with her head, nodding toward nothing in particular.

"What?" Quinn feigned ignorance. "Have we *what*?"

"You know," Bonnie repeated.

"What are you talking about?" Quinn couldn't help but smile. "Tell me, Bonnie, what? Say it."

"No, you aren't going to get me to say it."

"I'll tell you if you say it, but you have to say it."

"You know I don't like to say it. It's an embarrassing word, Quinn." Bonnie lowered her voice, "Plus, if my mom or dad heard me say that, I'd be in dutch real good."

Quinn continued, grinning as she slowly shook her head, "Not going to tell you..."

It was the kind of game Quinn could keep going for several minutes, especially on a lazy day like this. She loved to see Bonnie blush when she said the word, and it made Quinn laugh every time. Bonnie had an aversion to that particular word. Ultimately, Quinn would prevail, because Bonnie's curiosity was strong and her will was weak. It was just a question of how long it would take for Quinn to wear her down.

"So do you think it will rain tomorrow?" Quinn asked, intentionally changing the subject.

"You're a pain in the butt."

"C'mon, Bonnie, I know you can do it."

Bonne stood up and looked casually into the back door of her house to make sure her mother wasn't close by. She walked over to Quinn and through clenched teeth, barely moving her lips, puffed out the word, making it sound like "pphhhuck." Her face immediately flushed red, and Quinn howled.

Bonnie turned away, concealing her visceral reaction.

"What was that Bonnie?" Quinn howled. "Was that a duck fart I heard?"

Bonnie couldn't help but laugh. "You are about a stupid bitch sometimes," Bonnie said, shaking her head. "I don't know why you do that to me."

"HEY! Language, young lady!" came a voice from inside the house.

"Sorry, Mom," Bonnie tried to sound earnest, as Quinn futilely attempted to stifle her own laughter by plastering her hand tightly across her mouth. All this accomplished was to force Quinn to inhale through her nose and, in doing so, she snorted—twice, involuntarily in rapid succession. This sent Bonnie into convulsive laughter, and Quinn laughed so hard she had tears rolling down her cheeks.

"What is going on back here?" Bonnie's mother was at the screen door, a large woman wearing a royal blue muumuu with slices of watermelon imprinted randomly all over it. She looked quizzically at the two girls, not seeking any answers, just insuring nothing was untoward.

"Oh, nothing," Bonnie lied to her mother.

"Well, settle down, for heaven's sakes, girls." She shook her head and retreated further into the house, satisfied nothing catastrophic was occurring in her backyard.

The girls regained their composure, wiping the tears away and catching their breath.

"I guess I best be going, Bonnie." Quinn stood up.

"Whoa!" Bonnie said. "Not so fast. You never answered my question."

"Oh, yeah, that." Quinn sauntered down the sidewalk. "Yep, all the time."

CHAPTER 16

"Whose idea was this?" Sonny eyed Quinn suspiciously.

"Mine ... well, ours, together," Quinn replied. "He needs a steady paycheck."

Sonny sipped his beer, watching several bowlers roll at once, momentarily ignoring Quinn as the steady sound of the wooden pins crashing into each other created a sense of excitement in the packed North End Bowling Lanes. League night was a big deal here, and all twenty-four lanes were jammed with bowlers. Quinn stood patiently, waiting for an answer from Sonny, or at least some recognition of her request. She studied the new team shirts: button-up-the-front, red with black sleeves and a three-fourth-inch-wide, black, horizontal pocket band; a large scripted black "M" above the left breast pocket, accented by three differently-sized black, white, and red diamond-shaped patterns overlaid on one another on the shirt's right breast.

"Sonny!" Quinn pressed, trying to pull his attention back to their conversation.

"What? I'm busy here, Quinn." Sonny looked impatiently over at Quinn and then back to his teammates on the lanes. "I'm up in a minute." Sonny looked impressive in his new shirt, which complemented his jet-black hair and dark complexion.

"Will you at least think about it?"

"Yeah, okay," Sonny relented. "Just tell Charlie to come see me tomorrow, and we'll discuss it man-to-man."

"Okay." Quinn turned to walk away and caught Sonny's impatient eye. "Thanks."

Sonny simply nodded as he lifted the bottle to his lips.

Quinn walked outside and got in the passenger seat of Charlie's waiting car as it idled with Charlie behind the wheel in the no-parking zone.

"Well, what did he say?" Charlie asked before Quinn had even closed the door.

"He didn't say no. He said you should come talk to him tomorrow without me," Quinn replied. "See, I told you."

"Hot damn!" Charlie punctuated his excitement with a quick slap of the dashboard.

"Just play it cool with him," Quinn warned. "You think you know him, but I know him better. If you are too eager, it's going to cost you something, more than if you just act like it's something you might be interested in."

"Yeah, okay, but this could be the break we need. If he can get me in at the railroad, we could get married and have a place of our own!"

Quinn smiled, touching Charlie's face. "I know. And I want that, I do. Just be careful with him. You know how he is. He's going to want something in return for doing you a favor."

Charlie put the car in gear and pulled away from the curb.

"I'm no fool, Quinn," Charlie said. "He won't get over on me. I can keep helping him out with the other stuff, but I just need a steady job. He's been around, he knows that. Any good man knows this stuff."

"Well, if he knows it, why do we have to even go begging to him?"

"Because, he's a busy man. He's got a lot of irons in the fire. You wouldn't understand. Let me handle it."

Quinn looked out the side window of the car at the passing night, rolling her eyes at Charlie's remark. *This could be a real turning point,* she thought as Charlie sang "Autumn Leaves" with Nat King Cole on the car radio. With steady income, Charlie could support her and they could afford a place of their own. Marriage would change her world, for the better, she was sure of that. How hard could it be to keep house, make dinner, do some laundry? She loved the thought of having babies to care for. She thought of her baby, who would now be walking and trying to talk at two years old, and again replayed in her mind's eye how pretty she was. Quinn imagined a richly furnished home, with happy parents doting over the child, and an older brother—the perfect family of four. It made her sad. And happy. If only she could see her, just to know how she was doing and that she was okay. But she was lost somewhere out there. Forever.

Quinn looked forward to moving on, and she knew having Charlie's babies would help her put the past behind her. She worried about Sonny's hesitation tonight. *Was he actually going to help Charlie? Or did he not want me and Charlie to get married?* Sonny was a hard one to figure out.

Quinn's thoughts pulled on her, dragging her into the familiar territory of unwanted questions and answers and non-answers. *How could I get free of Sonny? Why do I keep torturing myself by reliving the past? Why do some people always seem happy? What's wrong with me?*

"Quinn!" Charlie shouted her name, causing her to jump.

"What? Why are you yelling?"

"I called your name three times. What are you thinking about over there?"

"Nothing, really," Quinn lied, trying to conceal her moodiness. "Just thinking about us getting married, I guess."

"Let's get some beer and go park at our spot." Quinn knew what Charlie meant. She wasn't in the mood for sex tonight.

"Fine." Quinn forced a smile. "Let's go."

Charlie smiled and turned the radio up a bit louder. He reached over and rubbed Quinn's thigh. She looked at him, placing her hand over his.

"I love you, Charlie," Quinn said, mustering sincerity.

Charlie pulled up to the curb in front of O'Banyons, a small neighborhood carryout.

"I'm coming too," Quinn said. "I want some gum."

As they walked into the market and approached the counter, Quinn saw another couple speaking to the owners. The woman held a toddler, dressed in pink. Quinn fought her mind's attempt to take her back to that dark place. She couldn't help but smile as the little girl's green eyes locked on her. Uncomfortable, she said hi to the child and then exaggerated her smile as she opened her eyes wide. The girl giggled, as did Quinn. Charlie purchased a six-pack of Pabst Blue Ribbon and a pack of Juicy Fruit, and they returned to the car.

"Charlie, did you see that baby in there?"

"Cute kid," Charlie said nonchalantly.

"Wouldn't you like to have a baby like that?"

Charlie was quiet for a moment, blankly looking at Quinn. It was a question he never expected to be asked.

"Well, yeah, someday," he finally said. "Of course, that's all part of getting married … sure." He said the words slowly, as if he were working out the answer to a difficult math problem.

"Really, Charlie? Do you mean it?" Quinn asked. "Do you think we'd be good parents?"

"Of course," Charlie replied, this time without hesitation. "You'll be a good mom, and I'll bring home the bacon."

Charlie glanced over at Quinn, to be certain he hit all the right points, as he drove to their spot. He contemplated getting laid. Quinn chewed Juicy Fruit, contemplating motherhood.

CHAPTER 17

1958

"Hey, Quinn," said the familiar voice through the telephone receiver. "What are you doing?"

"Hi, Bonnie. I've got my hands full tonight."

"What's wrong? What's all that noise I hear?"

"I've got my brothers and sister here, and that crying is, of course, Thomas, who is hungry."

"Oh, how'd you end up with a house full?" Bonnie asked.

"Mom's in the hospital. Slit her wrists," Quinn said quietly, cupping her hand over her mouth and the phone. "Sonny knocked up Karen Clemens, and Mom and Sonny had it out. After Sonny left, Mom tried to kill herself."

"Oh my God!" Bonnie exclaimed. "Is she okay?"

"Yes, she's fine. She didn't hit an artery. She got some stitches, and they are keeping her for observation tonight. Hold on a minute." Quinn held the receiver away from her mouth. "Kids—quiet down. Mary, please feed Thomas for me. I'll be there in a minute." Quinn replaced the phone at her ear. "Sorry, Bonnie, I'm going to have to go."

"Is Charlie there with you?" Bonnie asked.

"No, he's working at the rail yard. Got a twelve-hour shift tonight."

"Okay, then. I'm coming to help," Bonnie said. "I'll be there in twenty minutes."

"Really? That would be great. I'll put some coffee on. We can get these kids fed and settled and then catch up."

True to her word, Bonnie arrived shortly. Thomas was playing on the floor, surrounded by the three older kids: seven-year-old Mario, five-year-old Mary, and four-year-old Gino. Thomas, Quinn's only child, was eighteen months old. He studied Bonnie with his big, blue eyes as she walked into the room.

"Bonnie, thank goodness you're here. I just realized I need to get milk. Can you watch the kids while I run over to the store?" Quinn asked.

"Sure. We'll be fine." Bonnie settled into a chair, watching Thomas watch her. "He has his father's blue eyes, Quinn, that's for sure."

Quinn smiled. "Yep, little Charlie. I won't be gone long." She looked at her siblings. "You three be good for Aunt Bonnie."

Quinn walked the two blocks to O'Banyons. It was a pleasant summer evening, and dusk was still a couple of hours away. This was Quinn's favorite time of year and the best time of day. She enjoyed the break in temperature as the sun receded from the sky, cooler but still warm enough to walk outside without a jacket.

The bell above the market's screen door announced Quinn's arrival as she pulled it open. The spring snapped the door shut behind her. Quinn heard children's voices and turned to see two small girls playing in the corner with the canned goods. One was a towhead, the other dark-haired. The girls chatted noisily, oblivious to the world around them. Quinn thought the girls looked to be about five years old and assumed they belonged to the friendly man and woman who worked here every Saturday night.

"Good evening," the dark-haired man greeted Quinn. "Can I help you?" He peered at her from behind black horn-rimmed glasses, a broad smile on his face. Quinn couldn't help but like the nameless man. His wife appeared from the small office, smiled and nodded as she walked toward the girls in the far corner.

"I just need a half-gallon of milk tonight," Quinn replied.

The man turned, opened a shiny steel door on the refrigerated case behind him, and placed the glass milk container on the countertop. As he rang up the sale, Quinn pulled her change purse out of her pocket. The voices in the corner grabbed her attention.

"Eva and Jennifer, it's time to put everything away." Quinn loved the name Jennifer. It was the name she would have given her baby girl. She also liked Eva and had never thought of that name. It was one you didn't hear much. As Quinn completed her purchase and said goodbye to the gentleman, she heard the girls chatting cheerfully as the cans clanked onto the shelves.

"Eva, put these two together," one little voice commanded.

"No, they don't go there," Eva responded.

"Yes, look, they match," retorted Jennifer.

"Well, I like it here," Eva insisted.

Hmm, a squabble might be brewing, Quinn thought. As Quinn left through the screen door, bell jangling, she heard the mother, a voice of intervention, speaking quietly to the girls. Their voices faded as Quinn's footsteps carried her away from the store. She found herself wondering about the family. Why were they only there on Saturday nights? What were their lives like the rest of the week? Did the man work all week somewhere else and then spend Saturday night working at O'Banyons to make extra money? And why was his wife always there? Why didn't she just stay home with the kids so they didn't have to play at the store?

Quinn walked into her house to find Thomas asleep in Bonnie's arms. The three older kids were playing with Thomas's toys, obviously bored. Mary, with her perpetually sad eyes, looked up at Quinn and said, "I'm hungry."

"I know, Mary, I know. I'm going to make your supper right now." Quinn hustled off to the kitchen, and soon the sounds of pots clanking, water running, and dishes being moved about announced dinnertime was near. Bonnie, still holding Thomas, walked quietly into the kitchen as Quinn filled the plates for the three kids. Hot dogs, baked beans, and cooked carrots greeted the three hungry children as they settled at the table.

Bonnie sat down in an empty seat, refusing the food. "No thanks, I ate before I came. I will take a cup of coffee though." Quinn poured her a cup and set the steaming black liquid in front of Bonnie.

"Want me to take him?" Quinn asked, nodding to the slumbering Thomas.

"No, he's fine," Bonnie whispered, kissing Thomas's forehead.

As the kids finished their meal, Quinn told them to start their baths and change into their pajamas since they were staying the night. Bonnie took Thomas to his playpen and gently laid him down. He squirmed until he got comfortable once again, then slept on.

Bonnie and Quinn worked together to clean up the kitchen, as Quinn periodically checked on the bath progress with the three kids.

"I'll finish up in here," Bonnie said, standing in the kitchen, "if you want to get the kids settled in."

"Perfect," Quinn said. "Be back in a few minutes."

Quinn hustled the children into their pajamas and tucked them into a makeshift bed on the floor of Thomas's room. Soon, all three were soundly asleep. Quinn retrieved Thomas, who was now awake, bathed him, put him in pajamas and, after letting him play for another hour on the floor of the living room, put him to bed for the night. At 10 o'clock the house was finally. Quinn settled into the threadbare beige couch, and Bonnie sat in the matching beige rocker with her feet on the vinyl-covered, red ottoman.

"Going from one kid to four in one day is exhausting," Quinn said as she pulled a Chesterfield cigarette from its pack.

"Mary is a quiet child," Bonnie said. "Is she okay?"

"She's been like that for the last several months," Quinn said out of the corner of her mouth, the other corner occupied with an unlit cigarette. She looked at Bonnie as she struck a paper match, put it to the cigarette, inhaled, and then blew the match out as she exhaled the cigarette smoke.

"Something doesn't seem right," Bonnie said. "She just seems sad."

"Well, I am sure all the drama going on over there with Mom and Sonny has had an effect on her," Quinn said. "Those two are like oil and water."

"So tell me about this whole thing," Bonnie said. "Sonny told your mom he got Karen Clemens pregnant?"

"Oh yeah, she shouldn't have been surprised. Mom pulled her out of Sonny's car by her hair three years ago, remember that?"

"Yep." Bonnie chuckled. "Sonny denied everything, right?"

"Sure, that's what Sonny does. Mom should have known better, but, no, she just plays right along, anything for Sonny." Quinn put the cigarette to her lips and puffed, exhaling the smoke through her nose.

"What do you mean? 'Anything for Sonny'? He's always treated her like crap. I would think she'd want to get rid of him."

"It doesn't work that way," Quinn eyeballed her friend. "Do your mom and dad get into fights?"

"You mean real fights or just arguments?"

"Either. I mean, do they go at each other all the time?"

"Oh, no," Bonnie said, surprised. "I mean, they might argue once in a blue moon, but it's not often."

Quinn contemplated her friend's answer. Her mind flashed briefly to the little family at O'Banyons.

"Huh," Quinn said, almost to herself. "So how do they work out problems?"

"Well, I don't know. It's not like they have a lot of problems to work out, I guess."

"What do they argue about, then?"

"Dad may want to go fishing on a weekend instead of doing some chores around the house, that kind of thing. Not much, though," Bonnie said.

"Does your mom get mad when your dad comes home late?" Quinn asked.

"Come home late? He never comes home late—you mean from work?"

"Well, from being out," Quinn explained.

"No, he doesn't go out. He goes to work, comes home, we have dinner, and then Mom and Dad sit together in the living room and read the paper, ordinary stuff like that, you know."

She didn't know, but Quinn nodded as if she understood.

Footsteps were heard on the porch just before the front door opened and Charlie appeared in the room.

"Hi, Honey," Quinn said.

"Hello, Charlie," Bonnie said, almost at the same time.

"Hi you two." Charlie put his lunch pail down on the small table in the living room.

"Make me some food, will you?" Charlie looked at Quinn, expressionless, his request more of a demand than a question. "I have to get cleaned up, and I want to eat before I have to go out."

"Where are you going?" Quinn asked.

"Out," Charlie said, trying too hard to sound important. "I have business to take care of."

Charlie started up the steps to the second floor.

"Please don't wake those kids up, Charlie," Quinn called after him, in a hushed voice.

"I best be going, Quinn," Bonnie said as Charlie disappeared up the stairs.

"Thanks for coming tonight. I'll call you tomorrow." Quinn looked at Bonnie as she moved toward the kitchen. She jerked her clenched fist with an outstretched thumb toward the stairs and quietly said, "I've got to go fix Prince Charming's dinner."

CHAPTER 18

The ringing phone demanded an answer. Quinn put Thomas in his playpen, stepped across the toys on the floor, and grabbed the receiver.

"Hello?"

"Cops are on their way over there, Quinn." It was Sonny's voice.

"What? Cops? Why?" Quinn asked, her mind racing. "What are you talking—?"

"Shut up and listen to me," Sonny said quietly, evenly. "Charlie's in jail, and the cops are coming over there with a search warrant."

"In jail! What happened?" Quinn tried to comprehend what Sonny was telling her.

"I'll explain it later. Listen, when the cops get there, don't say anything to them. Don't answer their questions. Nothing. Just let them in and let them search. They won't find what they're looking for, so don't argue with them."

"Why's Charlie in jail?" Quinn's concern was slowly turning to irritation. "What the hell is going on, Sonny?"

"Listen-to-me-now!" Sonny barked, never raising his voice. "I will explain later. But do not say anything to the cops. Nothing! Do you understand?"

Quinn was silent for moment.

"Quinn!" Sonny snapped. "Do you understand?"

"Yes," Quinn said quietly. "I understand."

"Good. Call me as soon as the cops leave."

"Okay. In the meantime, figure out how you're going to get my husband out of jail." Quinn slammed down the receiver without waiting for an answer.

Within minutes there was a knock at the front door. Quinn went to the door and saw two men. Both were dressed in dark suits, one with a blue tie and the other with a black tie, standing before her as she opened the door.

"Mrs. Charlie Freund?" the taller of the two asked, holding up a folded white paper in his hand.

"Yes?" Quinn sounded surprised.

"I'm Detective Sidner, and this is Detective Webb. This," he paused, holding the paper a little higher, "is a search warrant for this residence." The detective handed Quinn the paper, which she opened but didn't read.

"Come in," Quinn said calmly as she stepped back and fully opened the door, allowing the officers to enter.

"Are you the only one here?" asked the shorter detective, Webb.

"Just me and my son." Quinn motioned to Thomas in his playpen.

"This won't take long," Sidner said, looking around. "But we will need to search the entire residence. "Sit down here in the living room while we look around."

Webb walked to the basement door and said, "I'm starting down here."

Sidner bounded the steps to the second floor. Quinn could hear him as he moved between the two bedrooms above. Within a few minutes he descended the stairs, empty-handed.

"Do you know what we're looking for?" he asked Quinn.

"No, I have no idea," Quinn replied. "Do you?"

Sidner shot her a stern glance. Quinn stared back at the man, contemplating Sonny's instructions.

Webb reappeared from the basement, locked eyes with Sidner and shook his head slightly, almost imperceptibly. Webb began opening doors and drawers in the hutch in the small dining room, his back to Quinn. Within a few seconds he turned around, a silver transistor radio in his hand. He held it up in front of him, eyebrows raised as he looked directly at Quinn.

"Where'd that come from?" Sidner asked.

"I've never seen that before in my life," Quinn said. "Is that a radio?"

The two detectives looked at each other and then back at Quinn, sporting expressions of exasperation.

"Tell me why I shouldn't arrest you right now," Webb said impatiently to Quinn.

Sidner held his hand out to his side slightly to caution Webb. "Look," Sidner said, his tone softening, "we don't think you did anything wrong, Mrs. Freund. But we have a job to do. This is stolen merchandise. It would be better for all concerned if you were truthful with us about this radio."

"I've honestly never seen it before," Quinn replied. "I didn't know it was in there. I don't know anything about it."

"Okay," Sidner continued, "do you think your husband may have brought it home?"

"I don't know." Quinn looked directly into Sidner's eyes.

"Okay, fine," Sidner said. "We are taking it with us, and we'll turn this over to the prosecutor who will determine if there will be any charges against you."

Quinn felt her face flush and her mouth go dry. She was confused about the search and what was going on with Charlie, but she wasn't confused about the fact that Sonny definitely played a role in all of this. A big one.

"Why are you here? Why my house?" Quinn asked.

"Because we are investigating a crime, and your husband has been implicated. He's currently downtown at the city jail," Sidner replied as he scribbled in his pocket notebook. He tore out the page and handed it to Quinn. "Call this number and the clerk will tell you if he has bail set yet."

The officers left the residence with the transistor radio.

Quinn immediately dialed the number Detective Sidner gave her. After a few minutes, the clerk came back on the line and told Quinn that Charlie could be released on five hundred dollars bail. Quinn swallowed hard, thanked the clerk, and hung up. She then called Sonny, who answered on the first ring.

"The detectives are gone," Quinn said. "Bail is five hundred dollars to get Charlie out."

"What'd they find?" Sonny probed.

"Nothing," Quinn said flatly.

"Nothing?" Sonny paused. "Well, that's good." He was unable to conceal the surprise in his voice.

"Well," Quinn confessed, "not nothing. They found some little transistor radio, but I don't think it amounts to much." Quinn couldn't believe Sonny took the bait. Things were beginning to make sense now.

"A radio? Just a radio?"

"Yes."

"I'll go bail Charlie out. I'll bring him home in a bit."

CHAPTER 19

“Just do what your lawyer tells you,” Sonny advised, looking sternly into Charlie’s eyes, one hand on his shoulder. “I’ve got more experience in these things, so trust me, I know how to best get it over with.”

The two men sat facing each other in the small room outside the courtroom, waiting to go before Judge Davis for final sentencing. Neither man’s attorney had yet arrived. Charlie was clearly nervous, having difficulty sitting still. Sonny tried to calm him.

“You can’t change anything now. They caught you red-handed with the evidence.”

“That’s bullshit, Sonny,” Charlie protested. “I never took that radio. I had no idea it was in my house or how it got there!”

Sonny waved his hand nonchalantly by his face. “Look, water under the bridge. I believe you, Charlie.”

“That’s all they got on me.”

“Listen, we go in there, we plead guilty, we get thirty, maybe sixty days in lockup, and it’s over,” Sonny guaranteed. “We’ll be in there together, it won’t be so bad. It’s local time. We’ll play cards to pass the time. Three hots and cot. No big deal.”

“What about our jobs? Quinn’s pregnant again. V[illegible]out feeding my family?” Charlie asked, desperation in his voice.

“I’ve got it covered. Quinn won’t have to worr[illegible] we’re in the can.”

The door opened and Sonny’s attorney, Arn[illegible] in. Sonny stood and shook his hand.

“Arnold,” Sonny said, “this is Charlie [illegible] nervously and shook Bowerman’s hand.

"Oh, yes," Bowerman said. "Charlie, good. Your attorney is tied up in a hearing downstairs. He asked if I could cover for him for the plea today."

Charlie, surprised, looked at Sonny, who nodded his approval.

"Well, I–I guess … if that's what he said," Charlie stammered.

"Today is perfunctory, Charlie," Bowerman said, turning his full attention to Charlie. "No reason to be concerned. It's not like there's any real preparation for this, as there would be if we were having a trial or hearing. We're just going to stand before the judge, enter the plea, answer his questions, and then listen as he pronounces sentence."

This did little to calm Charlie. "Do you think he'll go easy on us?"

"I don't think you have a lot to worry about," Bowerman said, "but of course I can't predict what he'll do."

The courtroom door opened, and the bailiff called out Charlie's name.

Charlie and Bowerman entered the courtroom and stood before Judge Davis. After the clerk read the charge, the judge asked for Charlie's plea.

"Guilty, Your Honor," Bowerman's voiced boomed throughout the courtroom.

Judge Davis peered at Charlie over his reading glasses. "Mr Freund, do you understand that by entering a guilty plea, you are waiving your right to a trial by your peers?"

Charlie looked at Bowerman, who nodded.

"Yes, Your Honor," came Charlie's reply.

"And are you entering this plea voluntarily and without having been promised anything in return for this guilty plea?" Judge Davis sounded bored, like he'd said the same things thousands of times, to thousands of defendants.

"Yes, Your Honor."

"Okay, Mr. Freund, before I pronounce sentence, I have one question for you. Consider your answer carefully," Judge Davis said, looking directly at Charlie. Charlie shifted nervously on his feet.

The judge continued, "Mr. Freund, standing before the court today, are you willing to disclose the name of the person who orchestrated this crime?"

"A moment, Your Honor?" Bowerman interjected, looking at Judge Davis. The judge nodded. Bowerman leaned over and whispered in Charlie's ear. "It's a trick question. He wants to see if you will take full sponsibility for your actions. Don't name anyone else; instead, tell him e solely responsible." Bowerman straightened up. Charlie looked at his legs trembling and heart pounding.

"Well?" Judge Davis asked.

"Your Honor, I take full responsibility for what happened," Charlie began. "I acted alone."

"Well, well, well. Now isn't that interesting, Mr. Freund, that you would come into my courtroom, pleading guilty to a crime, attempting to sell the court on your remorse." The judge's voice rose as his face reddened. "Yet when given the opportunity to come clean with the facts, you lie, right here in front of God and everybody!"

Charlie's mouth dropped. "But, I … I … no, Sir, … I …" he spluttered.

"But what?" Judge Davis thundered. "I know there is a codefendant in this case, young man! So don't come in here and tell me you acted alone when all I have to do is look at the facts before me to see that you're lying!" The judge paused, writing on the papers before him for several seconds before looking up again.

"The court hereby finds you guilty of the charges of receiving stolen property and grand larceny and sentences you to a period of confinement of one year in the state penitentiary." Judge Davis banged the gavel. "Next case!"

Charlie felt the judge's gavel right between his eyes. The sheriff's deputy came from the front of the courtroom, yanked Charlie's hands behind his back, and cinched handcuffs down snugly on his wrists. The cold steel was a shock to Charlie's clammy skin. The deputy roughly shoved Charlie onto a wooden bench near the thick double doors.

"Sit here, Charlie," the deputy instructed. "I'll take you down for booking after the next defendant is sentenced."

Charlie watched as Sonny entered the courtroom with Bowerman at his side. He looked confident and strong. *How does he do that?* Charlie searched Sonny's face for an expression, a hint that he recognized something had gone wrong with his plan. Sonny apparently didn't notice Charlie sitting there in handcuffs. *What a cool customer he is,* Charlie thought. *He's in for a big surprise.*

Charlie listened as Judge Davis repeated the exact words to Sonny regarding his plea. Sonny responded each time as Charlie had, with "Yes, Your Honor" at the appropriate cue.

Judge Davis then asked Sonny if he acted alone in the commission of this crime. Charlie noticed Bowerman didn't have to whisper in Sonny's ear.

"Your Honor, I want to be truthful with this court," Sonny began. "So the truth is I did not act alone in the commission of this crime. As you know, Charlie Freund was also involved in this incident."

"Well," Judge Davis drawled slowly, looking over his glasses at

Sonny, and then beyond, locking eyes with Charlie. "Finally, a defendant willing to speak truthfully before the court. Thank you."

Once again, the judge took to writing for several seconds on the paperwork before him. He then leaned forward in his chair.

"The court finds the defendant guilty as charged of one count of receiving stolen property and one count of grand larceny. I hereby sentence you to five years' probation. You are to report to the probation officer for details and conditions of your probation." The judge banged the gavel before announcing, "We are adjourned."

Charlie watched as Sonny shook Bowerman's hand. It appeared they were sharing a laugh. Sonny turned, and Charlie caught his eye. Sonny gave a slight shrug and then approached the deputy.

"Do you mind if I have a word with Charlie?" Sonny asked.

"It's fine, Sonny, but make it fast," the deputy said. "I've got to get him down to booking."

Sonny put a hand on Charlie's shoulder, bending down to speak to him.

"What the hell happened?" Charlie blurted out.

"Got me," Sonny said. "Bowerman said you got a year? What did you do to piss off the judge?"

"I guess I answered his question wrong." Charlie stared blankly at the front of Sonny's shirt, still dazed by the whole encounter.

"Listen, don't worry about anything at home. I will make sure Quinn has money to live on. Anything she needs, okay?"

"Damn, Sonny," Charlie said slowly, reality settled in. "My baby will be born before I get out of the pen."

"Don't worry about that." Sonny sounded earnest. "I will make sure Quinn has everything she needs. I'll be there to visit you too."

"I've never been in jail before," Charlie said. "I've heard bad things."

"Look, kid, you're tough." Sonny put his face directly in front of Charlie's, looking deeply into Charlie's eyes, his voice a whisper. "I'll make sure you're protected. Just don't worry about anything. You'll be out before you know it and everything will be fine."

"What about my job?"

Sonny gave a curt nod. "I'll handle that. I'll get a leave approved. Your job will be waiting when you get out."

"Thanks, Sonny. I appreciate everything you do for me."

CHAPTER 20

"I promised Charlie I would take care of you while he's away," Sonny said, waiting for some response from Quinn.

Quinn said nothing, staring blankly at Sonny, one hand on the doorknob of the partially opened front door, her small frame blocking the entrance to her home. Thomas peeked around her legs.

"Why don't you invite me in so we can discuss the arrangements?" Sonny asked. "I have some money for you."

Quinn's eyes searched Sonny's face briefly, then to the activity on the street behind him. She was turning his words over in her mind. Her eyes burned from the bright sunlight—something she hadn't seen much of in the past seven days. Charlie's sudden incarceration had turned her world upside down. She looked at Sonny. He raised his eyebrows slightly, gesturing toward the door.

"C'mon in," she said with resignation in her voice.

Sonny flashed a smile, but Quinn ignored it and turned around, picked Thomas up, and held him in her arms. Sonny followed Quinn to the living room. She sat in her beige rocker; he sat on one end of the couch. Thomas was content on his mom's lap.

"I have money to get you through the rest of the month," Sonny said, eyes fixed on Quinn. He leaned forward and fished a white envelope out of his back pants pocket. He held it up and waived it slightly. "There's a hundred bucks here. That should get you through the month." Sonny put the envelope on the end table beside him.

"Why?" Quinn's face hardened, eyes aflame.

"Why what?" Sonny foolishly asked.

"Don't give me the 'why what' shit, Sonny," Quinn said quietly. The firmness in her tone and manner surprised Sonny and even herself.

"You know what I am talking about. Why did you set Charlie up to take the fall? And don't deny it—this is me you're talking to. I know you, and I know how you think."

"Set up? Are you kidding?"

"Do I look like I'm kidding?" Quinn spat the words at Sonny, never taking her eyes off of him. "Charlie may not have figured it out, but I know." Quinn paused for effect, watching Sonny watch her. "And you know that I know."

"So?" Sonny shrugged his shoulders, bored with the conversation. "What to do about it now? We make the best of a bad situation, and Charlie will rebound when he comes out of the can. I'll make sure of it."

"That's your plan? Charlie needs to go back to work and stay the hell away from you when he gets out."

"Don't be so bitter, Quinn," Sonny cooed. "It will all work out, you'll see. In the meantime, you and I need to make the best of it."

Quinn's eyes narrowed. "Oh?"

"I'll take care of your living expenses ... unless my money is no good here." Sonny enjoyed the gamesmanship.

"I'll take your money, don't you worry about that," Quinn said. She hated him and his money, but she knew she had no choice. The question was how much this money was going to cost her. Sonny always had a price.

"I thought so. I am a man of my word, Quinn. You know that. I promised Charlie I would do this."

Quinn ignored his comment. "When should I expect another envelope? Rent is due in two weeks."

"I will pay your rent directly to your landlord, so you don't have to do anything. Give me your utility bills, and I'll pay those too. All you need is money for groceries. It will be better that way."

"You're enjoying this, aren't you?" Quinn lobbed the question across the room.

Sonny smiled. "I'm just trying to make things simple for you. Just trying to be helpful. I can take care of your needs while your husband is away."

He paused. "All of them."

Quinn sat Thomas on the floor to play. Her expression relaxed as she drilled into Sonny's eyes with hers. She spoke clearly and calmly. "You don't scare me anymore, Sonny."

"I've never tried to scare you, and I've never thought you were scared of me."

Quinn rolled her eyes and looked away, saying nothing.

"I don't want you to be scared of me now, Quinn. I'm trying to help you out here. There's no reason we can't help each other, is there?"

"Like I said, I know you. You don't care about helping me."

"Sure I do. That's why I am taking care of you financially. It's what fathers do for their kids."

"Fathers? Did you really just say that? You're not my father!"

"That hurts." Sonny sounded sincere. "I have always thought of you as my own daughter."

"Fathers don't do what you did," Quinn said flatly, the first time in her life her mouth formed any words about "it" to anyone, anywhere. She surprised herself. Suddenly, she felt a surge of something within her. Something clicked. Something good.

"Quinn, that is something special between us. Something we shared that we both wanted." His expression held no hint of gamesmanship, sarcasm, or deception.

"You don't believe that!" Quinn retorted, feeling the heat of anger rush to her face. "Even you couldn't possibly think that!"

"I know it," Sonny said calmly. "You were a special child, and we had a special bond."

"Stop it!" Quinn shrieked. Thomas looked up, startled, and began to cry. Quinn picked him up and put him to her shoulder, rocking him slightly while patting his back to calm him.

"You are making too much of that. It was no big deal," Sonny said. "It's a family matter."

"No big deal? If that's true, why did you always drive me to confession?"

"It's part of our religion, of course. It's all part of our heritage, from the old world."

"What are you talking about, Sonny?"

"Children must learn from their parents the ways of the world. This is just part of growing up."

Quinn was dumbfounded. She pondered this explanation, but her mind spun in tumultuous circles. Was she overreacting? Maybe she is the person who doesn't fit in. But it didn't make sense—the secrecy Sonny always demanded.

"I don't believe you," Quinn responded finally.

Sonny's expression was almost tender. Quinn needed time to think. She felt a sense of mild relief, but at the same time her mind was in turmoil. She would kill him right this moment if she had the means. She hated this man, and she hated that she hated him. She looked back at Sonny, who was looking at her with innocence.

"Just stop it," Quinn said calmly. "Don't say anything else. Leave the money and leave me alone."

"Quinn?" Sonny did not making any movement to take his leave.

"What?" Quinn said, a little less venom in her voice. She felt her anger dissipate slightly. Maybe she was being too harsh. Could she have misjudged Sonny? She'd never seen this side of him. He looked so vulnerable. Why would he think she wanted him to do that to her? Was it something she said or did? Was Father Schaefer right—had she tempted Sonny or provoked him in some way? In many ways it seemed so long ago; yet it also seemed like it was just yesterday.

"I just wanted what was best," Sonny said softly. "I knew I couldn't take the place of your real father, but I did my best to prepare you for the real world. That's all."

Sonny stood up to leave, leaned over and kissed Thomas on the crown of his head as he nestled quietly against Quinn's breast. Sonny looked down at Quinn as he straightened up.

"I'll take care of you, Quinn," he said, "like I always have. Even though you are grown up and your mother and I are divorced, you and I will always be family. Always."

CHAPTER 21

"He tried to kill himself," Bonnie said.

"Are you sure?" Quinn asked. "That doesn't sound like something Sonny would do."

"I saw the chart. He's admitted for anxiety tension state, which is the medical term for a nervous breakdown."

Quinn and Bonnie sat on Quinn's porch, watching the early August evening pass. Quinn held two-month-old Matthew in her arms while Thomas played on the front sidewalk with his cars and trucks. Quinn was baffled. Sonny always seemed to be in complete control of everything. What went wrong? If it had been anyone else telling her this, she would be certain they were wrong. But Bonnie was a registered nurse and had access to the records, and she wouldn't lie to Quinn—there was no reason for her to do so.

"Is he okay?" Quinn turned to her friend while reaching for a cigarette. "Is he going to live?"

"Oh, yeah." Bonnie waved her hand. "He didn't take enough to kill himself."

"It's not like Sonny to miscalculate," Quinn stated.

"In my experience, people who want to kill themselves stick their head in a gas oven. That's a sure way to do it. Or blow their brains out with a gun. Drug overdoses are a cry for help."

Quinn contemplated Bonnie's comments. "Have you seen him?"

"Yes. I've seen him every day since I work on that ward."

"How long will he be in there?"

"Probably for another week at least."

Quinn studied Matthew's sleeping face before glancing up at Thomas on the sidewalk. She thought for a moment, furrowing her brow slightly. "Can he have visitors?"

"Yes. As a matter of fact, Father Schaefer comes at least once every day, sometimes several times."

"He does?" Quinn asked. "Does he get any other visitors?"

"Just his probation officer. Two o'clock sharp every day."

"What do those two talk about?"

"Mostly the guy is giving Sonny crap about violating his probation. Did you know Sonny's not allowed to even be in a bar, much less manage a bar?"

"No, I didn't know that." Silence settled over them. Quinn was deep in thought as they sat together watching Thomas run his dump truck loudly along the sidewalk, accompanied by his best imitation of an engine and screeching brakes.

* * *

The next day Quinn left the boys with her mother and drove to the hospital. Upon checking in at the visitor's desk, she was informed only two people could visit at a time and both passes were in use for Sonny. She elected to wait. Shortly, Father Schaefer appeared and handed his visitor's pass to the receptionist. He spotted Quinn.

"Hello, Quinn," he said, his voice taut. "Nice to see you."

"Yes," Quinn replied, "nice to see you too, Father." It was a lie, a violation of the eighth commandment.

"Are you here to visit Sonny?"

"Yes. Do you know who is with him now?"

"His probation officer. Perhaps you should wait about twenty minutes and they should be finished, then you can go on up to see him."

After a few meaningless pleasantries, Father Schaefer said goodbye and walked through the lobby and out of the building. Quinn immediately approached the visitor's desk, signed out the pass, and proceeded to Sonny's floor. She entered the double doors to the psychiatric ward and saw Sonny and another man sitting in the dayroom talking. She walked over and stood beside Sonny. The other man stood up. Quinn stuck her hand out, introducing herself.

"Hi, I'm Quinn, Sonny's daughter."

Sonny looked at Quinn, puzzled, but managed to say hello.

"I'm Bill Goodman," the stranger said curtly.

"He's my probation officer," Sonny explained.

The two men continued talking as Quinn quietly scrutinized Sonny. His hair was disheveled, he hadn't shaved, and the hospital gown and cotton robe he was wearing looked to be a size too small.

"Look, I've been pretty lenient with you, but things are going to change when you get out of here," Goodman said.

Sonny looked at Goodman, waiting for him to continue speaking.

"The terms of your probation clearly say you have to report to Father Schaefer every week, you are not to have any alcohol or drugs in your system, and you cannot be in any liquor establishment." Goodman took a breath. "That includes your family's bar, and it means you can't work there, let alone manage it."

Sonny looked down and started to speak.

"I manage it," Quinn interjected. Both men looked at her. Sonny squinted slightly as he studied her face.

"Oh? Is that right?" Goodman asked, looking at Sonny.

"Yes, that's right." Sonny labored at sounding casual.

Goodman's face telegraphed his skepticism. He looked first at Sonny and then rested his eyes on Quinn, searching for a deceptive cue in her expression. "So tell me a little about it."

"What do you want to know?" Quinn asked, sounding confident.

"Let's start with compensation," Goodman said. "How much is Sonny paying you to run the bar?"

"One hundred and twenty-five dollars per week." Quinn looked at Sonny and smiled. He returned the smile, but his eyes were stern. "And I get a quarterly bonus of five percent of the gross revenue if we hit our margins."

Goodman eyed Sonny suspiciously. "Is this true?"

Sonny shrugged his shoulders and said, "Yeah." He looked at Quinn and forced a smile.

"So you will have payroll records to substantiate that she's running the bar, right?" Goodman's eyes were locked on Sonny.

"Well, not yet," Quinn offered. "It's only been three weeks, and my first monthly check isn't for another week. Do I have that right? I get confused on the dates." Quinn arched her eyebrows at Sonny.

"Yes, that sounds about right," Sonny replied on cue.

Goodman looked at Sonny, then at Quinn, and then back at Sonny. "Listen, pal, if you're lying to me on this and you don't produce the payroll records to back this up, I am going to violate you and you will end up doing hard time. I'm done playing around with you, do you understand?"

"Yes sir," Sonny said, a tinge of contempt in his voice.

Goodman got up, excused himself, and left Quinn and Sonny alone. Quinn sat down in the chair previously occupied by Goodman.

"What was that all about?" Sonny demanded.

"I just saved your ass, that's what it was all about."

"How am I going to cover this story with Goodman? You heard him; he'll violate me."

"I wouldn't want you to be violated, Sonny," Quinn said with a deadpan face. "I am going to run your bar. There's nothing to cover."

"You can't run a bar," Sonny replied, disgusted. "What do you know about running a bar?"

"What I don't know, you're going to teach me. I can do this. I *am* going to do this." She looked directly into Sonny's eyes, waiting for his resistance.

"Why would you think I would stand for this?" Sonny's face flushed. "Who do you think you are, coming in here and telling me what is going to happen?"

"Who do I think I am?" Quinn said evenly. "Let me tell you who I am. I am the person who is going to save you from the law and from yourself. I am going to save you, even though God knows you don't deserve to be saved. And not only am I going to save you … I am going to make money for you at that bar. I am the person you have to rely on now, or you will lose your bar."

"Do you think I need you?" Sonny blurted out.

Quinn leaned forward in her chair, resting her elbows on her knees, looking directly into Sonny's face. She spoke quietly. Sonny leaned forward so he could hear her.

"Do you need me? You have no choice, Sonny. I'm the only game in town right now. This is the best deal you are going to get. Understand something … I'm not asking permission. I'm telling you how it's going to be. Unless you want to join Charlie in prison, then, yeah, I guess you win. But assuming you want to stay out and make money, this is what you are going to do."

Sonny looked dejected. Quinn knew—and Sonny knew—she was now in control. He looked at her, confusion etched on his face, quiet emotion in his strained voice as he struggled to form the word: "Why?"

She looked at him and smiled sweetly. "Because we're family."

CHAPTER 22

With each step Quinn put distance between herself and Sonny, who was sitting in the dayroom staring blankly out the window. Her legs felt increasingly wobbly as she walked into a new, strange world and put the familiar, old world behind her. The realization of what she had just done finally smacked into her consciousness; what had been both a fantasy and a plan, reinforced by angry braggadocio and nonsensical self-talk during her solitary drive to the hospital, had somehow inexplicably evolved into action. Action that involved other people—Sonny, the law. *For God's sake, the law,* she thought.

That probation officer scared the crap out of her. Quinn felt her stomach flip-flop, as her mind raced with the details. She felt sweaty, her heart raced, and her lungs demanded fresh, cool air. Her legs felt weighted, heavier with each step. The eyes of everyone she passed in the hallways watched her, not understanding her. Somehow strangers knew what she had done. Their looks were accusatory, judging her for her deceit. She wanted to turn around, go back to Sonny, make things right.

How could she already miss the world of familiar misery she had just left behind?

Bursting through the door, Quinn felt the hot sun and humid air hit her face. Beads of perspiration broke out on her forehead, nose, and neck. She felt queasy as she approached her car and leaned on the fender. Her stomach lurched; cold sweat beaded around her lips. She fought the urge, but suddenly the burning pushed up through her stomach into her throat. She doubled over and spewed vomit, heaving with such force that it splattered onto the fender and tire of the car. After a few minutes, her belly surrendered and she stood up. The smell was putrid, as her partially digested lunch baked in the sun on the hot asphalt. Quinn grabbed her purse from the trunk deck of the car, opened the door, and wearily flopped into the driver's seat.

The car was even hotter inside than the pavement outside. Quinn retrieved a tissue from her purse and wiped her mouth. She cranked the driver's side window down, then slid across the seat to lower the passenger side window. Cooler air began moving across the interior of the car. Quinn pulled more tissue from her purse and patted her forehead and face dry. She sat staring through the windshield, her mouth filled with the taste of bile, her throat burning. Around her the noise of the city filled the air. A car horn sounded, another blared in response. Diesel trucks shuttered past the parking lot, their engines revving as they shifted gears. Children chattered as they ran through the parking lot with parents calling after them to slow down, be careful. Dogs barked, trains rumbled, birds chirped and squawked.

Quinn heard none of it. She sat, and she watched, and she thought.

Fifteen minutes passed before she returned. She started the car and leaned forward to look into the rearview mirror at herself. A wry smile grew across her face.

* * *

"Good afternoon," the kind gentleman behind the counter called out as Quinn entered O'Banyon's Market.

"Hello!" Quinn smiled.

"What can I help you with today?"

"I'm working off a list today, but I think I can find what I need."

Quinn walked the aisles of the small store, filling her basket with the necessities for tonight's supper for Thomas and Matthew. She heard the two girls, fixtures in the store on Saturdays, playing somewhere close by.

"I'm white, I'm Catholic, and nobody in my family is divorced," Quinn heard one little voice say. Quinn rolled her eyes, annoyed.

"Me too," said the other girl, and both giggled.

Quinn rounded the corner by the bread and saw both girls playing with boxes of pasta.

"Hello, girls!" Quinn said.

Both girls looked up, but neither said anything. Quinn quietly moved on. *Quite the little brats,* she thought.

"Eva, Jennifer," called the man. "Come here." Quinn heard the shuffle of the girls' feet across the wooden floor, followed by the man's voice, speaking low but still filling the tiny store.

"When someone speaks to you, it is impolite to ignore them," he admonished the girls. There was silence before he continued. "You should always say hello to anyone you meet because you never know, that might be the one thing that will make them have a great day. Understand?"

"Yes," one of the girls replied.

"Okay, now go say hi to the nice lady."

The patter of four feet announced the impending arrival of Eva and Jennifer before Quinn. She smiled and looked at the two girls standing before her, realizing how much they had grown.

"Hi," they said in a singsong chorus.

"Hi, girls," said Quinn. "How are you this evening?"

"Fine," said the green-eyed girl.

"We hope you are having a great day," said the brown-eyed, dark-haired one, smiling. The green-eyed blonde was more serious, studying Quinn's face.

"Well, I hope you are having a great day too, thank you!" Quinn continued shopping.

Eva and Jennifer, relieved of their burden, happily scuffled back to the pasta shelf and resumed their activity there, with an intensity and seriousness appropriate for seven year olds.

Quinn approached the counter to check out, setting her items down as the man behind the counter smiled.

"I'm sorry for that," he whispered. "They know better."

"Oh, it's nothing," Quinn said, with a wave of her hand toward the man. "I've got two of my own. I understand. Those girls are getting big. I feel like I've watched them grow up."

"Yes, it's amazing how fast time passes," the man said. "They're both seven now."

"Oh? Twins?"

"No, no, cousins. One is mine, the other is my wife's brother's child. My wife was an O'Banyon."

"All this time I thought they were sisters."

"Might as well be. They're very close. And alike in many ways," the man said, laughing.

"I guess it's all in the bloodline," Quinn joked.

CHAPTER 23

1964

"You need to talk some sense into your wife." Sonny turned up his collar against the wind. The clank of a coupler rattled in the distance as small amounts of snow spit through the gray air. The rail yard was still buzzing with activity, despite the bitter cold wind.

"You know how stubborn she can be," Charlie said, shoving his gloved hands into the pockets of his heavy coat. He shifted from one foot to the other.

"Oh? So you're saying you can't control your own wife?" Sonny chided.

"No, of course not, that's not what I am saying. I'll take care of it."

Sonny turned to view the activity behind him. He glanced at his watch. "Twenty minutes to go, and we can get out of here."

"How soon can you take the bar over?"

"By the first of the month. My hearing is on the twenty-fourth, so if everything goes like it's supposed to, my probation will be satisfied and I'll be completely released. I want to get her out of my bar and get back in action again."

"I get it. I'll make it happen," Charlie guaranteed.

Sonny looked at Charlie. "You sure you can handle her without any issues?"

"Issues? What are you talking about?"

"She knows what goes on there. I can't have her running her mouth about it because she got fired."

"Naw, nothing to worry about there," Charlie said. "I'll make sure of it. She needs to stay home with the three kids anyway. With Douglas only being a year old, she should be there with him more."

"Yeah, kids need their mom at home," Sonny quipped.

"Sonny, how about this," Charlie said cautiously. "What do you think about not calling it a firing but she's resigning instead?"

Sonny looked at Charlie. "Why? What makes the difference?"

"I just think it's easier for her to say she quit than to say she was fired, that's all." Charlie kept his eyes on the black yard engine working the cars back and forth as the next train was built.

"I don't care, whatever," Sonny grunted. "I just want her gone, understand?"

"Yep."

* * *

"I'm not surprised," Quinn said as she placed a fresh cup of coffee in front of Charlie. The shiny new Chromcraft table, with its red top, chrome legs, and matching red, vinyl-padded chairs gleamed in the light of Quinn's kitchen. The table was one of the many things Quinn was able to purchase with the money she made from the bar. Now it was all about to come to an end.

"We can make it on what I bring home from the railroad."

Quinn wasn't listening, knowing this was Sonny's cowardly way of dealing with the inevitable. After all, it was no secret that someday his probation, with its restriction on his liquor activity, would end. Quinn had no illusions about his intention to get rid of her.

"You should stay home with the kids anyway." Charlie studied Quinn closely. "You are taking this better than I figured you would."

Quinn lit a cigarette, pulling the ashtray toward her. She sat back in her chair. "Sonny had it pretty good these past five years. I ran that bar and made him money, and all he had to do was keep his nose out of it. It's too bad he isn't smart enough to see that."

"Now, Quinn, I don't think it's that he isn't smart enough. It's that a man wants to get back behind the wheel, be in charge of his own destiny, that's all. That's understandable."

"Whatever you say," Quinn smirked.

"Well, I say you're staying home with the kids, and that's all that matters."

"I know, honey, it's fine," Quinn said softly. "If that's what you want, it's fine. I will stay home and take care of the kids and leave you to bring home the bacon."

"Well, there's more to this, and I'll be making more money for us."

"How's that?"

"Sonny bought another building, by the bar, and he's going to start a discount store."

"Why is he doing that?"

"He thinks he can make more money by retailing the stuff from the rail yard instead of fencing it out of town," Charlie explained. "I don't know all the details, but he said it will mean more money."

Quinn shook her head. "I think you need to be careful. We can't afford for you to go back to prison. Don't trust him."

"I can trust him. Regardless of what you think, I know what I am doing. It'll be fine."

Quinn looked at Charlie, her face softening.

"What?" he asked.

"I'm pregnant."

CHAPTER 24

1968

"Sorry I'm late, girls," Mario Lupo hustled into the sanctuary, where fifteen-year-old Eva and her cousin Jennifer sat twirling their hair in their fingers, chatting about the important topics of boys, school, and makeup.

"It's okay, Mr. Lupo," Jennifer said.

"Let's get started, shall we?" Mr. Lupo took his place and spread his music on the stand in front of him. "Eva, will you play the piano and, Jennifer, you do the organ for this one, please?"

The girls climbed the three steps and took their appointed places. Eva's blond hair, flowing halfway down her back, caught Mario's attention. He watched as she sat at the piano, nodding she was ready. Mario looked at Jennifer, who was staring at him intently from the organ.

"Which song do you want to start with?" Jennifer asked.

"*Adoro te Devote*," Mr. Lupo said absentmindedly.

Eva looked puzzled and shot a glance at Jennifer, then back at Mr. Lupo.

"Oh, sorry, girls! *Godhead Here in Hiding* is what you have in your sheets. *Adoro te Devote* is—"

"Latin!" Eva interrupted.

"Very good!" Mr. Lupo smiled broadly, his dark eyes sparkling. He looked at Jennifer, who just giggled slightly at her cousin's obvious play for Mr. Lupo's approval.

Mr. Lupo nodded, and Eva and Jennifer began playing. The smooth fluidity of the organ soothed the more abrupt notes of the piano, combining to fill the sanctuary with auditory beauty. Mr. Lupo closed his eyes, waiting for the right moment to begin singing.

"Godhead here in hiding, whom I do adore …" his pitch-perfect baritone voice blended melodiously with the accompaniment, like a thick, warm liquid that flowed reverently into the sacred space, filling it with feeling and emotion that should only be experienced, not described. Jennifer's hands caressed the keys of the organ as her feet worked the pedals in perfect synchronization. She loved accompanying Mr. Lupo. She pretended it was only her and Mr. Lupo, alone, creating this beautiful music. She was smitten with everything about him. He was tall, dark, and handsome. He had a way about him, which attracted her. She stole a glance at him as he continued singing, his face in earnest and reverent expression, eyes closed, open mouth forming the words perfectly.

"Bring the tender talk true of the Pelican, Bathe me, Jesu Lord, in what thy bosom ran—Blood whereof a single drop has power to win …" Mr. Lupo opened his eyes briefly as he continued singing. Jennifer quickly shifted her eyes back to the score in front of her, never missing a note. Mr. Lupo finished the song, smiling as Jennifer and Eva held the last notes.

"Nicely done, girls!" Mr. Lupo was pleased. Eva smiled brightly at him.

"I have a question," Eva spoke up from the piano.

"Yes?" Mr. Lupo arched his eyebrows.

"Is that a misprint, or is it supposed to say 'pelican' in that one line?"

"No, that's not a misprint."

"Oh, okay," Eva stammered, looking at Jennifer, who shrugged.

"Let me explain this, girls," he said. "It has an important meaning. As you know, this is a Eucharistic song, and I'll be singing it as Father Schaefer distributes the host during the Sacrament."

Both girls nodded in agreement, eyes firmly fixed on Mr. Lupo as he continued. "And, of course, the sacrament of communion symbolizes the body and blood of Christ, which cleanses us from sin. So you probably think, okay, but what's a pelican got to do with this, right?"

The girls giggled in unison.

"You see, in medieval times, Christians believed the pelican had a unique way of feeding her young if there was no food to be found." Mr. Lupo watched the two girls to see if they were listening. "She would puncture her own chest, her bosom, and feed her babies with her blood as it flowed from the wound."

"Really?" Jennifer said. "That seems extreme."

Mr. Lupo smiled and gave a slight chuckle. "In nature, mothers are especially protective of their young and will do whatever their instincts direct them to do to protect and nurture their babies. It's the way the species survives."

The girls contemplated this for a moment.

"So, okay, the mother pelican feeds her babies her own blood," Eva started, "but why is that in this song?"

"Well, think about it," Mr. Lupo said gently. "What saves us from eternal damnation in hell?"

"Jesus Christ," Eva automatically blurted. She had learned from a young age that when in doubt about the answer to a question from a religious authority, Jesus Christ was the correct answer, or would at least get you by.

"How?" he pressed

"By dying on the cross," Jennifer offered.

"Sure, and what did he shed on the cross for us?"

"His blood. Of course! Now I get it!" Eva exclaimed.

"Right," Mr. Lupo said, looking from Jennifer to Eva, "and in the bigger picture, the pelican sacrificing her blood for her young is symbolic of God sacrificing his son, Jesus, on the cross, to atone for our sins."

The room was quiet for a moment as Mr. Lupo's words sunk in.

"But you said it was in medieval times," Eva challenged. "Does a pelican do that or is that just a myth?"

Mr. Lupo thought for a moment before answering. "Does it matter?" he softly questioned.

"Well, yes, I think it does," she replied. "If we base our beliefs on something that isn't true, then how can we know what we believe is true?"

"Ah, good question, Eva! What about you, Jennifer, what do you think about all this?"

Jennifer furled her brow. "I think a lot of things don't make sense on earth. Someday when we are with God in heaven, we'll understand."

"What do you think, Mr. Lupo?" Eva asked.

"I think faith is the belief in something without facts to prove it. I, personally, believe I am a child of God, saved by the precious blood of Jesus, who died on the cross to save me from my sins, and someday I will be in heaven with him, freed from my sin and the darkness of this world." Mr. Lupo paused to take a breath, watching the girls closely. Satisfied they both comprehended what he was saying, he smiled broadly as he slapped his knee with his hand. "So, in the grand scheme of things, it doesn't matter how a pelican feeds her kids."

The girls giggled, looked at Mr. Lupo, then back at their music.

CHAPTER 25

"Finish your lunch and you can go back outside and play," Jennifer coaxed the three young children.

She glanced at Eva, busily washing dishes, attempting to get a head start on the task they had put off after breakfast.

"We should have soaked these dishes," Eva grumbled.

"Egg yolk?" Jennifer already knew the answer.

"Yes. It gets stuck in the forks."

Jennifer laughed, causing Eva to look up from her labors.

"Oh shut up or you can do it!" Eva giggled.

"We're done," eight-year-old Gerald announced. He held up his hands, which were coated with grape jelly and peanut butter. Jennifer grabbed a cloth, wetted it, and wiped his hands and face. Then she turned to Bobby, seven, and did the same. Ten-year-old Mark held out one open hand, palm up, indicating his expectation to be treated with enough human dignity to clean off his hands without the help of a girl.

Jennifer walked the boys to the back door and saw the four neighbor boys playing in the yard. "Look, boys, your friends are waiting for you."

The neighboring family was a family of five boys: Thomas, eleven, was the oldest; the remaining brothers were Matthew, Douglas, and Randall, ages nine, eight, and six, respectively. Little eighteen-month-old William was the fifth. Jennifer enjoyed watching the kids playing on the swing set and in the sandbox of the backyard. It was quite a group, all boys, no girls, and most days they played in the summer sunshine until night fell and they were exhausted. As she leaned against the doorframe, her mind wandered to her own childhood, how she and Eva played much the same way. Wagons, tricycles, bicycles, and games. Hopscotch, jacks, hide-and-seek. *Summer seems to just fly by when you are a kid,* she thought. In two short weeks it would be time for a return to school—her first year of high school.

"Hey, ninny," Eva's voice called from the kitchen. "Did you get lost?"

"I'm coming," Jennifer replied, knowing Eva wanted her to dry the clean dishes. She reluctantly grabbed a dishtowel and began working on the pile of dishes in the drainer. The seven boys playing in the backyard created a continuous wavelength of sound, migrating steadily through the open windows. The girls had honed their child-rearing skills such that they could tell what was happening with their charges just by listening, almost on a subconscious level.

Suddenly the auditory stream-of-consciousness was pierced by a single word, emanating from a young male voice. Jennifer looked at Eva, incredulous. Eva's forehead was stretched high as her jaw dropped, her lips forming a perfect "O." The world went silent. Someone in the backyard of this home, situated in this little Midwestern community, brought the world of mothers and babysitters to a screeching halt, a final moment of tranquility before the inevitable chaos and consternation uncontrollably ensued.

"Who said that?" Jennifer whispered, panic-stricken.

Eva started to giggle but put her forearm to her mouth. "I didn't know any of them even knew the f-word!"

"Oh, this isn't good," Jennifer said as both girls headed to the back door. As they burst through it, seven pairs of eyes looked innocently at them, but no one said a word. The two youngest, Randy and Bobby, looked up from the sandbox only momentarily, with casual interest.

"Who said that?" Eva demanded. The conspiracy of silence lasted but a brief moment. Several fingers pointed at Matthew, but Thomas, the oldest of the group, hands at his side, looked at Jennifer and Eva, committing to nothing.

Eva homed in on Matthew. "What do you have to say?"

"It wasn't Matthew. It was one of the smaller kids. I think it was Gerald." Thomas affixed the blame firmly.

"What's going on out here?" Mrs. Freund appeared suddenly from her back door, carrying little William.

"Well, someone said a bad word … a *really* bad word," Jennifer explained.

Mrs. Freund threw a glance at the kids. "What word?" she asked.

"The f-word," Eva responded. "Everyone says it was Matthew, except Thomas, who says it was Gerald."

"You kids get inside," Mrs. Freund snapped. Her children

immediately hustled silently into the house. She walked closer to Eva and Jennifer.

"Inside," Jennifer commanded. She wasn't sure why, but it seemed appropriate. She watched as the three boys sullenly filed into their house. Jennifer turned back to Eva and Mrs. Freund.

"Did you hear it?" Mrs. Freund asked.

"Yes, we both did," Eva replied.

"Well, which one was it?"

"We couldn't tell," Jennifer said. "We were inside."

Mrs. Freund shifted William to her other hip and sighed with exasperation. "Well, I will talk to my boys, but I doubt they would have said that word loud enough for anyone to hear it."

"Well, I don't think Gerald, or the other two, would say it all," Eva piped up, defensively. Jennifer could tell Eva was not far from mouthing off to Mrs. Freund but prayed silently she wouldn't.

"Oh? And how do you know that, Missy?" Mrs. Freund retorted.

Jennifer intervened. "Well, we don't, actually, but it would be the first time we've ever heard any of them say a dirty word."

"Well, there's a first time for everything."

"No, I don't think these three even know what that word is, so I don't think it was any of them," Eva said.

Well, Jennifer thought, *she's done it now.*

Mrs. Freund eyeballed Eva. "Well aren't you so cock-sure of yourself?"

"Look, I just know these boys wouldn't say that. This family doesn't use those kinds of words."

Jennifer knew Eva had just poured gasoline on a fire.

"You keep your kids in your yard, and I'll keep my boys in my yard!" Mrs. Freund spewed out her words, her anger like hot lava. What would they tell Linda, the boys' mom, when she got home?

"Fine!" Eva retorted. "We'll do that!" She turned and walked into the house, allowing the screen door to slam behind her.

"Look," Jennifer offered, "I'm sure it's a just a misunderstanding. We can work this out, Mrs. Freund."

"Well, she just thinks her shit doesn't stink, now doesn't she?" Mrs. Freund snapped.

Jennifer looked toward the back door and then at Mrs. Freund. "I'll talk to her and the boys. I am sure we can figure out what happened and get this settled once everyone calms—"

"We'll see about that." Mrs. Freund turned and walked into her house without looking back at Jennifer.

CHAPTER 26

Jennifer watched as the three boys played on the floor of the living room, occasionally glancing through the front window. Eva's absence today made the day seem to drag by. A week had passed since the "incident," as she and Eva now referred to it. Jennifer was happy things seemed back to normal. Nobody knew who said the word, but all was forgotten. Eva and Mrs. Freund had actually spoken and, while their relationship certainly wasn't warm, it was cordial enough that the kids could play together and there was no squabbling amongst anyone, including the adults.

Jennifer found herself wondering where the Freund boys were today. With Eva sick at home and the Freunds missing, it was just her and the three boys.

She glanced out the window and saw Mrs. Freund pull up to the curb in her big, wood-paneled station wagon. The boys were piled in the front and back seats. She watched as they got out of the car and opened the tailgate. Mrs. Freund pulled baskets of peaches out of the car, handing them to the boys to carry inside. Thomas and Matthew struggled with a bushel basket, as Mrs. Freund balanced her purse and William. Randy and Douglas at her side, she pointed to the two smaller baskets, instructing them to unload and bring them into the house.

As they turned to walk inside, an errant peach toppled off of Douglas's basket. He set his basket on the tailgate and dashed into the street, chasing the peach.

Jennifer immediately saw a flash of white and heard the screech of brakes. She couldn't see Douglas. Her heart sank, fearing the worst.

"Stay here boys! Don't you move!" She snapped and burst through the front screen door. Mrs. Freund's screams were shrill in the still summer air. The white car had stopped several feet from the station wagon, directly in front of Jennifer. Her heart pounded as she ran to the street, shimmying between two parked cars. She saw Douglas, motionless, lying on his side. Blood trickled from his ear. She bent down but was nearly bowled over by Mrs. Freund, still shrieking. Jennifer stepped back. She was struck by how peaceful Douglas looked, his expression of innocence contrasting with the blood forming a thin line from his ear to his neck, where gravity forced it downward toward the pavement.

Jennifer watched as Mrs. Freund wailed, bent over her son, calling his name.

"Douglas, baby, it's mom," she cried frantically, through her tears, patting his hand. "C'mon now, you're okay, c'mon now."

Jennifer became aware of people crowding around, nameless, faceless people who suddenly appeared. Mrs. Freund's cries of anguish indelibly etched into her brain, Jennifer looked around, waiting for someone to either wake her up or tell her what to do. So many people, but where was Eva, or her mother, or father, someone she could rely on to help her? She saw Thomas, Matthew, and Randy standing together, baby William in Thomas's arms. Thomas and Matthew's faces were pale, and Randy was crying. Jennifer remembered the children she left alone in the house and bolted for the front door.

Jennifer approached the steps to the porch and saw all three boys standing inside the screen door, bewildered by the confusion outside.

"What happened?" Gerald asked. "Why are all those people out there?"

Jennifer felt the sudden urge to cry, futilely trying to suppress her tears by wiping them away. They were relentless, causing alarm among the boys.

"What's wrong, Jennifer?" It was Bobby, putting her cheeks between his little hands as she sat down on the living room couch. He looked directly into her eyes, his face squared off with hers, his childish innocence and curiosity combining to force Jennifer to confront the harsh reality she had just witnessed. Worse yet, she would have to share it with these boys, who had done nothing to deserve this intrusion of real life into their perfect, happy world. *It's too much. I'm just a babysitter*, she thought. *I just wanted to make extra money this summer. What do I do? What do I say?*

"Boys, I need to call your mother," Jennifer said, wiping her face with her sleeve. "Let me do that, and then I will explain what is going on, okay?"

The boys, being the good, obedient boys they were, readily agreed.

But the silence in the house, silence where there was supposed to be noisy chatter, squabbling, and occasional yelling, was brutal and only emphasized the ugliness of the day. Jennifer made her way to the phone and called Linda. Through sobs and shortness of breath, she relayed what had happened to Linda, who promised to be home shortly.

Jennifer sat down on the couch again and pulled the boys close. Sirens pierced the afternoon as they drew close. "Listen, boys, something bad has happened," she started, taking a deep breath. "Douglas has been hit by a car."

Questions followed as Jennifer did her best to answer them. She dried tears from their eyes and hugged them, explaining again how important it was to stay out of the street. She told them she thought Douglas would be okay after the ambulance took him to the hospital. It was a lie, but she didn't care. She didn't know how to tell them the truth, and she convinced herself it was just her opinion that he was already gone. What did she know, anyway? She hoped he would be okay. But deep down, she knew Douglas was dead.

CHAPTER 27

"Girls, come sit with me," Mr. Lupo said quietly, summoning Jennifer and Eva from their positions at the piano and organ. Tears stained Jennifer's face. The girls sat down in the first pew of the church, and Mr. Lupo placed a chair in front of them and sat facing them.

"I know this is difficult." Mr. Lupo's kind voice echoed slightly in the large sanctuary.

"I ... I don't know if I can do this," Jennifer sobbed. She couldn't delete the images of Douglas lying in the street from her mind.

"It's okay, Jennifer," he said. "It's okay to be sad about this."

Eva, distraught but emotionally controlled, watched helplessly as Jennifer attempted to squelch her crying.

"I can play the organ," Eva offered. She looked at Mr. Lupo, who nodded slightly, indicating his approval.

"Girls, I want you to listen to me," he said gently. He paused, waiting for Jennifer to regain her composure.

Both girls looked at him but said nothing.

"Jennifer, Eva can accompany me for the funeral today, so you don't have to worry about that, okay?"

Jennifer nodded her head, as she wiped her face with a well-used tissue retrieved from her pocket. She had cried so much these past two days, she wasn't sure she would ever regain her sense of normalcy. It was too much to bear.

"Now," Mr. Lupo continued, "and more importantly, I want to make sure both of you are okay." He looked intently at Jennifer, and she saw his kind soul reflected in his dark eyes. She felt comfortable and safe with him, knowing he could somehow make this better.

"We don't know why God decided to take Douglas home. That's just part of the mystery of life. And it's normal for us to feel sad because we are going to miss him. But we must keep in mind that he is in a much better place with our heavenly father." Mr. Lupo searched the girls' faces for an indication that his words were having some effect.

"It's just not fair, though," Jennifer said, a hint of anger in her voice.

"Perhaps." Mr. Lupo nodded. "I learned a long time ago that life is not fair. It's one of the hardest lessons for us to learn, especially when we are young."

Jennifer glanced at Eva and then turned toward Mr. Lupo.

"I understand Douglas is in heaven and is better off now than he was here on earth," she said, "but the unfairness isn't about that. It's about how unfair it is to his parents and brothers. What about them?"

"I can't imagine how a parent feels, burying their child," Mr. Lupo said. "As a father, I can empathize and get some sense of how painful it would be to lose one of my children. As a matter of fact, I almost did once."

"What happened?" Jennifer asked.

"God helped me through that time," Mr. Lupo said. "So, no, I haven't had to bury a child, and it is terribly unfair and painful for the parents. But always remember, God has a plan, and it's not for us to understand it, but to accept it knowing, through our faith, that God always acts in our best interests."

"How can God allow this to happen and expect us to not be angry?" Eva piped up, her tone unashamedly irritated.

"It's not our right to be angry with God," a voice boomed from behind the girls. It was Father Schaefer, emerging from the back of the cavernous sanctuary. He casually approached the trio, his cold, blue eyes juxtaposed against the half-smile on his face. "God is omnipotent, and only he knows his perfect plan for us. Our job is simply to accept, by faith, our circumstances and live by his word."

Jennifer looked down, wishing the priest would just go away. Eva looked at the priest and nodded resignedly.

"You see, death is always the result of sin … original sin and our own sin," Father Schaefer continued. "And life comes from where?"

"From God," Jennifer automatically replied.

"Yes, from God, through our savior Jesus Christ. The good news is our earthly life may end, but we are saved from death by Jesus' sacrifice on the cross. So while we are sad Douglas was taken away from us here on earth, our prayers must focus on God, asking him to allow Douglas's soul to quickly pass through purgatory so he can live in God's presence eternally. To focus on our own grief is selfish. And pointless."

"Father, I am going to have Eva accompany me today," Mr. Lupo said.

"Oh?" Father Schaefer looked at Jennifer, who looked at him and shrugged. "Very well, whatever the three of you decide." He started to walk away, then stopped and turned around. "Jennifer?"

She looked up at the priest. "Yes, Father?"

"I want you to pray about this, pray for strength and for God's grace, and I want both of you to pray for Douglas's soul."

"Yes, Father."

Father Schaefer then looked at Mr. Lupo and waited until Mr. Lupo looked up at him before speaking. "Stop by my office in a bit. We need to go over some paperwork."

Mr. Lupo nodded. Father Schaefer turned and walked away, exiting the side door of the sanctuary.

"It will all be okay," Mr. Lupo said once the priest was gone. "Time heals these wounds, and in time you will mend and will have a better understanding of God's hand in all of this, if you so choose. In the meantime, it is important not to lose your faith. That's what Father Schaefer was trying to say."

Jennifer blew her nose, her eyes now dry. She suddenly felt exhausted.

"I won't lose my faith," Eva said. "But are you saying we can choose to heal or not to heal?"

"Yes, Eva," Mr. Lupo said, looking attentively at her. "That's what I am saying. You always have choices in life. You may not be able to choose how you *feel* right now, but you have the ability to choose your *actions*. The decisions you make today affect tomorrow, and eventually even a tragic death, like this one, can lead to a better tomorrow if we choose the correct path, God's path, one step at a time. If we make the right decisions, God will help us."

Mr. Lupo smiled at both the girls. "Remember this, girls. Every choice matters. In life, there are no little choices."

CHAPTER 28

Jennifer settled into the pew directly behind Mrs. Freund, who was holding William on her lap. Mr. Freund was seated to the left of his wife, staring straight ahead. Thomas, Matthew, and Randy flanked their mother on the right. Jennifer studied the back of Mrs. Freund's head, which bobbed up and down between sobs.

The sounds of Mr. Lupo singing *Ave Maria*, accompanied by Eva on the pipe organ, filled the stain-glassed space as bright midday sunlight beamed through each window. The beauty of the song was impotent against the dark, ugly reality of the day. Jennifer felt this was a phony spectacle that did nothing to ease the pain of the moment. But she knew her private thoughts could never be shared with anyone.

Father Schaefer approached the ambo, placing a few papers upon it before speaking. He surveyed the congregants, creating a sense of dramatic expectation before he spoke.

"We come today to worship our Lord, on this occasion of Douglas's passing from this earth. Why, we may reasonably ask, is such a young life taken from us … so tragically and so abruptly?"

Jennifer heard Mrs. Freund sob and, through her own tears, watched as the bereaved mother's shoulders involuntarily shuddered. Jennifer wiped her eyes and cheeks with a tissue, a futile effort to stem the flow.

Father Schaefer continued: "Let us be mindful of two things: first, death is the result of sin. But it doesn't end there, for those of us who are faithful know that ultimately the source of life is our God, who sent his son, Jesus Christ, to pay the price for our sins on the cross. Jesus' death and resurrection allow us to live with him in heaven for eternity. So Douglas's death is only an end in the earthly sense. Do we have a cause for mourning? Should we mourn his passing or rejoice in his eternal life in heaven with our Lord?

"In Jesus' own words in Matthew chapter 5, verse 4, 'Blessed are those who mourn, for they shall be comforted,' Jesus tells us all we need to know about this. In this context we, as believers are blessed, if we understand that Jesus isn't talking about happiness in the earthly sense of being blessed. He's talking about being blessed in the sense of a full and rich understanding of our spirituality, knowing that ultimately our happiness is the result of being in communion with God. Our grief, as expressed through mourning, for a true believer, is our grief over our sinful nature. Thus, we are comforted when we know if we live according to God's plan, all will be well, regardless of the tribulations, pain, and suffering we experience here on earth.

"So today, let us praise God and pray for the soul of this dear child, who passes into God's presence, achieving what all of us someday aspire to."

Father Schaefer extended his arms upward and outward as he concluded. "Today, as if on the wings of a bird, Douglas's soul ascends to heaven, and he is whole, no longer broken, no longer separated from his maker, but living in God's presence forever."

Muffled sobs, a rattling cough, and the restlessness of the imperfect mourners hummed steadily through the sanctuary as Eva began the recessional hymn. People shuffled out of the pews, stopping to lay a hand softly on the shoulders of the grieved parents to offer condolences. Mr. Freund nodded to each one, his face grim. Mrs. Freund sobbed in her tissue, disconnected and alone, estranged from the kindness of family and friends.

* * *

After forcing down a few bites of baked chicken and some green beans, Jennifer stood with Eva, talking idly in the church fellowship hall. The noise of the diners was beginning to diminish, as people finished their meals and said their goodbyes. The crowd was slowly thinning.

"Nicely done today," Mr. Lupo said, as he approached Eva and gave her a slight hug with one arm around her shoulders. He looked at Jennifer. "It was a lovely service, wasn't it?"

"Yes, it was," Jennifer replied. She didn't have any intention of sharing her real thoughts about the whole thing, especially with a religious man like Mr. Lupo.

"With that behind us, the healing can begin," Mr. Lupo said, his hands clasped together, accentuating his words with a slight flourish.

Mr. Freund approached Mr. Lupo, extending a handshake. "Sonny, thanks so much for everything today. It was beautiful."

"You're welcome, Charlie," Mr. Lupo replied. "Please let me know if you or Quinn need anything. And listen," he said quietly, "it does no good to blame her. Just be calm and let things settle down a little."

"Yeah," Mr. Freund said, looking uncomfortable. "I need to get her home. She needs to be away from here. All of this makes it worse for her."

Jennifer watched as Mr. Freund walked away. Mr. Lupo excused himself, leaving the girls alone once again.

"Blame her?" Eva said. "It's not her fault! I can't believe he's blaming her."

"That family seems to have a lot of problems," Jennifer said.

"Yeah," Eva agreed. "I don't understand people like that."

CHAPTER 29

1970

The rain on the window glass danced and sang to the beat of the wind as Quinn O'Connell's tears fell silently on the open Bible lying on the cold kitchen table in front of her. The psalmist screamed inside her head: "Behold, children are a heritage from the Lord, the fruit of the womb a reward." She lifted her glass and put the whiskey to her lips. It was seductively smooth, but even it was no longer her friend. It had long ago lost its ability to cauterize her anguish with temporary, sweet relief. She eyed the Valium tablets arranged neatly in front of her.

She looked up at the window and then through the glass and beyond, seeing all there was to see and yet seeing nothing at all. There was no meaning to be found there. There was only nothingness in a rainbow of gray. As she stared blankly she felt the familiar and heavy weight of sorrow, like a millstone around her neck, for the child she lost forever seventeen years before. Over time, the persistent throbbing of raw grief evolved into quiet, chronic despair. She felt despair metastasize to her feverish soul, consuming her humanity as if with a fire stoked by the Almighty's righteous fury.

After seventeen long years, Quinn had almost found God's forgiveness. She was unable to undo what she did and was not free to forget it. Eventually, she learned how to live with her painful memory and had moved on with her life. She even thought she was at peace with God. The pain of her loss was there, but the passage of time had proven the great healer of those wounds.

And then, in an instant, the price of forgiveness was levied upon her: Douglas.

For a time, Quinn sought answers. In time, she discovered her own truth about her God: "For the wrongdoer will be paid back for the wrong he has done, and there is no partiality."

With nothing left but the dancing and singing rain on the window glass, Quinn quit.

CHAPTER 30

1992

The phone rang, interrupting Quinn's Sunday evening. A woman's voice on the other end of the line asked if it was a good time to talk. Then came the question she thought would never be visited upon her, yet its inevitability was preordained.

"Did you give birth to a baby girl on November 24, 1954, in Norfolk, Virginia?"

Quinn's gasp broke the silence. The voice waited patiently for an answer.

"Yes," Quinn said quietly. She was unsure what to expect next.

"Your birth daughter has been looking for you. Are you willing to speak with her?"

"Yes," Quinn said without hesitation.

"I will have her call you tonight, then?"

"Please, yes." Quinn said.

Quinn went to the bedroom, where her husband of six years was preparing for bed.

"There's something I need to tell you," she said.

"Okay." Dave, a gentle man by nature, was curious at his wife's unusual behavior. "Now?"

"Yes, now. Sit down for a minute." She proceeded to tell Dave of her lost daughter, something not many people in her life knew about, concluding with the information of the recent phone call.

"Are you okay with all of this?" Dave asked, concerned.

"Yes, nervous." Quinn teared up again. "But all these years I have thought about her and worried about her, wondering what her life was like and whether she was okay. It all comes down to this, tonight."

The phone rang suddenly, intrusively, pregnant with possibilities and potentialities. Quinn's stomach flip-flopped as she hustled to the phone in the living room.

"Hello?" Quinn said.

"Hello, is this Quinn?" the voice asked.

"Yes."

"You gave birth to me thirty-eight years ago."

"Oh," Quinn breathed, tears flowing. "I've thought so much about you for so long. Thank you for finding me."

"I'm glad I found you, but I don't want you to feel pressured into meeting me. I will honor your privacy, if that is what you want."

"Where are you calling from?" Quinn asked.

"Right here in Louiston, Ohio."

"Do you live here?"

"Yes, all my life." She hesitated. "Except for three days in Norfolk, Virginia, after I was born."

The two women talked for thirty minutes, a mutual investment of time that satisfied curiosity and answered a few questions. Beyond that, it wasn't clear if this was going to be a simple moment in time wherein their lives would overlap but briefly or if this was the first thirty minutes of a long-term relationship.

"I am seeking medical information, history, for the benefit of my children. If you don't want to meet with me, or want anyone to know what I know, I will honor your wishes, but I do feel you owe me medical information." It was a daughter's request of a mother, in order to fulfill a mother's obligation to her children.

"I would like to meet you," Quinn said earnestly. "Can we meet in person?"

The women agreed to meet the following day at Quinn's apartment. Quinn placed the phone receiver in its cradle and went to bed. But sleep never came.

* * *

At 11:30 the following morning, the doorbell rang. Quinn opened the door. There stood her child. Her dark hair was colored with a red tint and styled in curls. Her green-gray eyes sparkled. She was beautiful. Quinn sensed familiarity.

"I'm Eva." She smiled, making her eyes dance.

"Come in!" Quinn exclaimed.

For ten full minutes they embraced. Tears, ever-tighter hugs, and more tears came. Finally they sat down, Quinn on the couch, Eva in a cushioned rocker. They spoke of their families and their lives. They caught up as much as was possible for thirty-eight years of separation. Both agreed the other person looked familiar.

"I grew up on North Elm Street," Eva said.

"I lived only a block from there on West Court Street," Quinn replied, "from '72 to '80.

"I grew up in the St. Joseph Parish and went to grade school there."

"That's it!" Quinn exclaimed, slapping her knee. "That's where I know you from! You used to have blond hair as a child and played the organ and piano!"

"Yes! Did you go to church there?"

"Not regularly," Quinn said, "especially after Douglas's death."

"Douglas?" A look of recognition overtook Eva's face. "Oh my God! You're Mrs. Freund?"

"Yes, I was until I married my current husband, Dave. Charlie and I divorced after Douglas died. Those were rough times. We remarried after the divorce, and then Charlie died suddenly a year later."

"Oh, I'm sorry to hear that," Eva said.

"It was a massive heart attack. Killed him instantly."

"So all of those boys … your boys … are my half-brothers," Eva said slowly, putting the jagged pieces of her life together. "I was actually babysitting my cousin's children while you lived next door, and my second-cousins were playing with my half-brothers, and I didn't even know it!"

Quinn let the impact of it all sink in. She removed her glasses and rubbed her right temple with two fingers, closing her eyes momentarily. Then, shaking her head, she smiled. "All of this time I thought you were somewhere in Virginia, and that I would never see you again. Ever. And here you were, literally in my own backyard!"

"How did you end up in Norfolk?" Eva asked.

"Back in the fifties, if you got pregnant, you went away to have the baby to avoid the shame and embarrassment to your family. I stayed with my aunt and her family until I had you."

"Did you get to hold me after I was born?"

"No." Quinn's eyes filled with tears again. "That was horrible. They felt it was best for the baby and the mother to be immediately separated so no bonding would occur." Quinn wiped her eyes with her hand. "What they didn't understand is that when you carry a baby around for nine months inside you, you've already bonded."

"I'm sorry," Eva said quietly. "It must have been hard, but I think it was brave of you to make the decision you made."

"Brave? I don't know about that," Quinn said, crying again, her tears tinged with a hint of anger. "Their attitude back then was 'give up your baby to a real home, and get on with your life.' They act like it's your decision, but when you're only thirteen, fourteen years old, you don't have any power to make any decision about that. You just have to do what they tell you to do." Quinn reached for a tissue and blew her nose.

"I can't imagine how painful that must have been."

"Most people, at least back then—but I think also even today—they don't realize the pain giving up your baby causes. And it never goes away. It's like you lose a part of yourself that you believe is lost forever. Anyone who hasn't experienced it cannot know how it feels."

"Well, the part you lost is back now," Eva said, smiling.

Quinn brightened, beginning to push away the old memories into the recesses of her mind where they belonged. She thought for a moment, then looked at Eva.

"Tell me about your adoptive parents," Quinn said.

"You mean my parents?" Eva shot back, a hint of irritation in her voice.

"Oh, yes," Quinn said tentatively. "Of course."

"My mom died in 1975," Eva said, her tone softening slightly as she saw the pained expression on Quinn's face. "My father is still living, and he is looking forward to meeting you."

Relief crept over Quinn's face. "I would love to meet him."

"He did tell me to tell you thank you for giving him the wonderful gift of a daughter," Eva said.

Quinn's eyes brimmed with tears, as her lips contorted into a painful smile.

"He also said to tell you that I was a spoiled, rotten brat!" Eva laughed.

Quinn laughed as she wiped the tears from her eyes with the well-used handkerchief she clutched in her hand.

"I have to go soon," Eva said. "My daughter is sick and I have a doctor's appointment for her at two o'clock.

"Who does she go to?" Quinn asked.

"Dr. White, a pediatrician here in town," Eva replied.

"I know who Dr. White is ... I was his medical assistant for five years back in the seventies."

"What? Eva said. "That means you actually gave your granddaughter her shots, measured and weighed her, all of that stuff."

The women looked at each other in amazement. Their lives were rejoined, but their paths had crossed many, many times in the past decades.

"I would like to spend more time with you, get to know you better, if that's what you want also," Eva said.

"Oh, honey, I do. I do."

CHAPTER 31

The landscape sped past them as Quinn drove down the narrow country road.

"There's another one," Eva said, pointing to the handwritten garage sale sign tacked to the telephone pole. "See? Straight ahead."

"They are back here in the sticks for sure." Quinn laughed. "Hopefully, that will mean some good deals for us!"

Eva sipped her coffee, watching for more signs. Suddenly, without warning, the farm fields and wooded lots on the left opened up into a yard filled with sundry items. Quinn smashed on the brakes, putting the car into a skid but still overshooting the driveway. The four people browsing through the sale looked up in unison. Eva laughed hysterically. "Way to drive it, Louise!"

"Shut up, Thelma," Quinn said, smirking as she put the car in reverse.

The two women hopped out and began the tactical maneuvering necessary to quickly survey another person's junk to identify potential treasures. Within five minutes they were back in the car, empty-handed.

"Well, that was a bust!" Quinn said. "All that detouring off our main route for nothing."

They backtracked to the state route, once again headed north to visit Quinn's mother, Roxanna, and Quinn's three half-siblings in Detroit.

Eva broke the silence. "I have a question for you," she said, looking over at Quinn.

"What's that?" Quinn asked, not taking her eyes off the road.

"Who's my birth father?"

Quinn stole a glance at Eva and then locked her eyes back to the road. "I knew that question was coming eventually," she said. "And I've thought about how I would answer it."

"What do you mean? Can't you just tell me?" Eva asked.

"I can tell you. But you need to understand the circumstances."

"Okay," Eva said slowly, not sure what would come next. "What are the circumstances?"

"I was sexually abused when I was young. Started when I was eleven years old. He got me pregnant when I was thirteen."

"Abused? Who was it?"

Quinn hesitated for a moment. "You know him. You grew up knowing him."

Eva's mind raced. "What? Who was it?" she demanded.

"Sonny Lupo."

Eva felt the shock wave of the words hit her, causing her mind to ripple with questions as it attempted to regain its equilibrium. She sank down into the leathered seat, oblivious to the hot coffee splashed on her hand as she fumbled with the flimsy cup that refused to go into the cup holder.

"Mario Lupo? From the church?"

"Yes, he was married to your grandmother, my mother."

Eva turned the information over in her mind, examining the implications of the revelation.

"I had a crush on him as a teenager," Eva said finally.

"Sonny?" Quinn, surprised, eyeballed Eva.

"Yes, I always thought he was good looking, always carried himself well."

"Hmm," was the sum total of Quinn's reaction to Eva's admission.

"Is that how I ended up back in Louiston?" Eva asked.

"What do you think?" Quinn shot back. "I am sure he had something to do with it."

"But you don't know?" Eva asked, searching Quinn's face.

"No, I don't know for sure, and I never suspected anything like that. He's way too slick for that, but there were other rumors about a sister's baby he arranged to have brought back."

"How could he pull that off?" Eva asked.

"Are you kidding? He's got all kinds of connections, and he's a manipulative sonofabitch. He can do just about anything."

"Connections?"

"Oh yeah, he's as crooked as they come. Always has been," Quinn said, disgust in her voice.

"Why do you say that?" Eva was trying to reconcile this person with the Mario Lupo she knew from childhood, the person who was still a prominent parish member and benefactor.

"He was in trouble with the law way back in the day, even before he was active in the church," Quinn explained.

"Okay," Eva replied. "But he's been religious and influential in the parish since I was a kid."

"So? That doesn't mean he's not a crook."

"But people can change." Eva suddenly realized she was defending Sonny. "I'm not saying what he did to you was justified or right, don't get me wrong. I'm just trying to understand him."

"Honey, nobody can understand him completely, trust me. I've worked for him, twice, and I probably understand him better than anybody, and he still leaves me scratching my head at times. Just know this, he cannot be trusted and you cannot believe anything he tells you. And as far as people changing? Oh, he changed alright."

"What does that mean?" Eva asked.

"When he was younger, he was a street thug doing stupid stuff and getting caught," Quinn explained. "As he got older, he got smarter and got some better connections. From where I sit, he just became a better criminal … more invisible, more of a behind-the-scenes mastermind. He got other people to do his dirty work for him."

"Do you think he's still doing that?"

"Sure! Why would he stop? He's greedy. He's always got something going."

"So you worked for him twice?" Eva's curiosity was unbounded.

"I ran his bar, Mario's, back in the early sixties for five years while he was on probation on a theft charge. Hell, he had cops on the payroll back then, for protection."

"Wow, really?"

"Oh yeah. Then once he was off probation and allowed to be back in the bar, he fired me and took back over himself."

"How'd you end up working for him after what he'd done to you?"

Quinn looked at Eva with the eyes of an experienced woman, one whose pathway in life was filled with low and long valleys, interrupted briefly by a few bright peaks.

"I learned a long time ago how to survive," Quinn said. "Sometimes you have to wallow with the hogs and suffer the shit before you can eat the bacon." Then she explained how she manipulated Sonny, using his probation officer in the process.

Eva laughed, admiring Quinn's spunk. "Were you scared?"

"Of course! Scared to death at first. That's probably what motivated me to do a good job."

"Weren't you angry when he fired you?" Eva asked.

"Not really. I was already pregnant, and Charlie was pressuring me. I never expected Sonny to keep me once he was off probation. See, you have to know how to align your expectations with reality, and then just figure it out from there."

"So when was the second time you worked for him?"

Quinn looked surprised, throwing a glance at Eva. "Well, now, of course!"

"He owns the Prospector? I thought you owned it."

"No, I just run it. He only comes around in the early morning, before we open. He stays in the shadows, and I make the business run."

"How'd you end up working for him this time?"

"Funny thing," Quinn said, "about change, that is."

"What's that?"

"Well, Sonny finally got smart. I always did well at Mario's. Made him a lot of money when I was there. As he got older and changed his tactics, he apparently realized he needed me to run the Prospector when he bought it. I think part of it is he knows I can make him money, but the other thing is that he believes he can trust me. Or control me."

"Can he?"

"Oh, he can trust me … but he'll never control me again. Ever."

"So how does that work between you two?"

Quinn smiled a wickedly evil smile, making Eva chuckle.

"What does that mean?" Eva asked.

"The trick to dealing with a control freak like Sonny is to make him feel like he's got all the control."

"And he doesn't?"

"Control is an illusion. I play on his need to dominate. I don't buck him on anything that interferes with his illusion of complete control, most of which is meaningless in the big picture anyway. But I watch for my opportunity, and I watch my backside. I can usually predict what he will say or do on any particular issue. But I never confuse predictability with trustworthiness."

She looked Eva straight in the eye. "Never."

CHAPTER 32

"She wants to talk to you," Quinn said, as she counted out the cash drawer. The Prospector wouldn't be open for paying customers for another hour, and she and Sonny were the only two people in the bar.

"What does she want?"

"I told her you are her father," Quinn snapped. "She wants to talk to her biological father."

Sonny was quiet. He appeared to be choosing his words carefully. "Am I her father?"

Quinn put the money down and looked at him, a look of incredulity on her face. "Of course you are … how promiscuous do you think I was at thirteen?"

"Your mother always claimed it was a child molester in the neighborhood."

Quinn resisted the urge to say, "It was." Instead she looked at him and said nothing, then went back to counting money. There was a long silence before Sonny spoke quietly.

"Can you ever forgive me for what I've done?"

Quinn responded without hesitation, "You're going to have to go a lot higher than me for forgiveness."

Sonny sat down on a bar stool, opposite where Quinn was standing, his sixty-seven-year-old legs tired. Quinn continued counting money, sorting and straightening the bills.

"Lay off the pull-tabs this weekend," Sonny said.

Quinn looked up, furling her brow but not saying anything as she counted silently to herself.

"Yeah," Sonny continued. "Word is the state liquor dicks are going to be in town all weekend."

Quinn finished counting the drawer and put it into the register. She placed a wad of bills into a green zippered bank bag and handed it to Sonny.

"Word couldn't get out, Quinn. My family and the people in the community ... they would have run me out of town."

"Yeah, I know what that feels like," she said, sarcasm dripping from her words as she grabbed a rag and a bottle of wood polish. She used circular motions to polish the bar briefly before stopping in mid-stroke. "How'd you manage to get her brought back here?"

Sonny, elbows resting on the bar, waved both hands slightly, as if trying to erase the question. Quinn stood motionless, staring at him.

"I know you had something to do with that." Quinn resumed her polishing.

"Your mother handled all the adoption paperwork. I ... I wasn't involved."

"That's bullshit and you know it," Quinn said flatly.

Sonny said nothing as he stared into the mirror at the back bar, inspecting the old man looking back at him.

"I wanted to make sure she was okay growing up," he said finally. "That's what a father does. He takes care of his own."

Quinn shook her head in disbelief. "Did it bother you to see her and know you couldn't tell her who you were?"

Sonny looked surprised. "No, why would it? I knew she was in a good home. I'm not so self-centered that I need her focusing her attention on me as a father. I gave her a good father and mother. What more could I do?"

"What about me?" Quinn asked. "Did you ever once stop and think about my feelings?"

"What? What do you mean? You wanted to give her up for adoption, so for you it was over."

"Over? Are you kidding me?" Quinn yelled. "Over? It's never been over for me. Never!"

Sonny sat up straighter on his stool. "Take it easy, Quinn," he pleaded. "What's all this about?"

Quinn looked at Sonny, fire in her eyes, her heart pounding. Thirty-eight years of pent-up rage billowed within her. She felt the hot flush of blood rushing to her face, her breathing intensified. She slowly resumed the circular polishing motion on the bar, saying nothing. She consciously forced herself to take a few deep breaths, bringing herself back into control. She continued polishing, focused on the bar top, with each stroke working her way down the bar, farther away from Sonny.

Finally, she brought calm within herself. She looked at Sonny. He was slumped over the bar.

"Sonny," Quinn called. He didn't respond. She ran to him, alarmed, grabbing his arm but got no response. She checked his breathing, but it was shallow. She was afraid to move him, for fear he would fall onto the floor, knowing she was not big enough to prevent the fall. His face was ashen—it was the same look she saw on Charlie's face when he suffered his fatal heart attack. Sonny, however, was breathing. Slightly, but breathing nonetheless.

"Sonny," Quinn said again, moving his arm slightly. He was dead weight. She knew he might die if he didn't get medical help soon. She glanced at the phone behind the bar, as she hustled around him. She stopped as she rounded the end of the bar, standing directly in front of Sonny's fading physical presence. She was just six feet from the phone. She looked at it, then back at Sonny. She listened. He was still breathing. She contemplated the quietness of the bar and the stillness of the man slowly fading on the end stool. She considered his death, what it would mean to the church, his coworkers, the neighborhood, the community, his family. What it would mean to her. Quinn looked again at the phone, which sat silent, willing to do its part if only asked. Suddenly she thought of Eva and immediately scrambled to the phone and frantically dialed 911.

A siren in the distance became increasingly louder with each passing minute. Quinn waited there, listening to Sonny's breathing, until she could hear it no more as two EMTs burst through the door of the bar.

She watched as they loaded Sonny on a stretcher. They listened with a stethoscope, checked his airway, and put him on oxygen. He was non-responsive. The second paramedic started an IV in his arm. The first EMT nodded to his partner after listening again with the stethoscope, and they hurried him through the front door. She heard the wail of the siren as the ambulance sped toward the hospital.

Quinn resigned herself to the fact that Sonny might survive.

CHAPTER 33

"The doctor said I can maybe go home tomorrow," Sonny said, looking up at Quinn from his hospital bed. His face was unshaven, his gray hair disheveled, and his skin lighter than normal. "Ten days in here is too much. I'm ready to go home."

"You're worn out, aren't you?" She asked.

"Yes, a little." His eyelids looked heavy. "They say it will be steady progress for about six months. My heart is damaged. Nothin' they can do about it."

"I don't know how long you were sitting there before I noticed you," Quinn admitted.

"Thank you for what you did for me. If you hadn't called for the ambulance, I'd have been a goner."

"Have you thought about what would happen if something happened to you?" Quinn was direct and to the point.

Sonny looked surprised by the question. "No, I'm not planning on anything happening to me," he quipped.

"Seriously, Sonny. Everything could be lost."

"You all would have to divide it up."

"It doesn't work that way, and you know it. Besides, I am not going to get into a pissing match with Karen."

"Well, she's my wife. I guess she and Roxanna will have to figure out what the kids each get. Duke it out," he joked, slowly shuffling his ham fists in front of him.

Quinn rolled her eyes. "There's something I want you to think about. Seriously think about."

"What's that?"

"Sign the Prospector over to me."

Sonny's eyes widened. "Why would I do that?"

"Because it's time for you, for once, to do something for me. By God, I've earned it. And it's not just for me, anyway. It's for her. It's the least you could do to leave something for her when you die."

Sonny contemplated Quinn's words. He hadn't thought about this before.

"This thing here," Sonny said, making a circular motion with his index finger in the air, "this whole ordeal—"

"What?" Quinn interrupted, sensing something different about Sonny in the way he was talking.

"This whole thing," he said slowly, "scared the hell out of me. I thought I was going to die a couple of times in the last week."

"You're lucky you didn't, Sonny," Quinn said flatly. "What would your legacy be if you had died?"

"I don't know. Haven't thought about a legacy," Sonny said.

"Well, you will leave a legacy. Everyone does, good or bad. Nobody gets to opt out. What would you want yours to be?"

Sonny bit the skin next to his thumbnail, thinking about Quinn's words. "I would want people to remember what a great guy I was and all the things I did for the church and the people in the church. I think that's important."

"I agree. It's important. What about your family, though? How do you want them to remember you?"

Sonny looked at her; his facial muscles relaxed and his eyes softened slightly as his eyelids blinked recognition. She had made her point.

"When we were at the bar, before your heart attack, do you remember what you said to me?"

"What?" Sonny asked.

"You said, 'it couldn't get out.' "

Sonny turned his head toward the window.

"A good legacy is a tricky thing, Sonny. Takes a lifetime to build one and five minutes to destroy it." Quinn stopped talking, studying Sonny as he gazed beyond the window. "My name is already on the liquor license, so technically I own it. Just give up your interest in the bar completely and let me have the real estate. Let me succeed or fail on my own, and let me keep the money I make."

After several minutes, Sonny looked at Quinn, his tired eyes ringed by large, dark circles against his sallow face. He pushed his lips together and set his jaw. Quinn looked into his eyes, unflinching, waiting.

"Maybe it's time for me to retire," he mumbled.

Quinn suppressed a smile. "It's for the best, Sonny."

"There are some things you need to know."

"What's that?" Quinn asked. "I've been running that place for fifteen years. I know it inside and out."

"You don't know all of it."

"Okay, tell me."

"There are some things you need to think about, beyond just the money you think you see going into my pocket." Sonny started biting his right thumb again.

"I know how much money goes through there every year, legal and illegal," Quinn replied.

Sonny's dark eyes flashed. "Yes, you do, but you don't see the big picture." He looked toward the door of the hospital room to make sure nobody had entered unseen. He lowered his voice, causing Quinn to slide the bedside chair closer and sit down directly next to him. She faced him and leaned forward, elbows resting on her knees.

"What is it, Sonny?" she asked.

"Certain arrangements have been made and have been in place for a long time. Those arrangements are commitments and must be honored."

"What are you talking about?" Quinn asked, although she suspected she already knew the general context of the answer he was about to provide.

"Not all the money that leaves the bar goes into my pocket. There are other people who have to be taken care of, so the bar continues to function as it should … uninterrupted."

"You're saying there's a payoff to be made," Quinn said.

"It's not just a payoff, it's continuing payments. A monthly expense. Think of it as an ordinary expense required to run a business."

"What are the payment arrangements? Who? How much? When?"

Sonny shook his head slightly. He stopped chewing on his thumb, pulled it from his mouth, and pointed his index finger straight up, holding it between his face and Quinn. "You don't pay anyone. I handle that, and nobody else."

"You want me to continue handing over money to you without knowing where it's going? How does that change anything?"

"It's a smaller amount you will be required to pay, the rest is yours to keep. And pay tax on, by the way." Sonny looked at Quinn. "I will need to make arrangements with the people on the other end of this, but I think I can sell it."

"What? Am I going to hand you cash every week?"

"Yes, I'll take it from there. It's better that way … you don't need to know the arrangements."

"And what happens if I decide to quit paying?"

"Then you better change how you do business. The money you make from selling pull-tabs, for one thing, will be gone because the state boys will catch you for sure. You could lose the bar."

"So this is protection money is what you're saying?"

"Think of it as an insurance policy. It's worked well for a long time. Don't mess it up. It's a small price to pay."

Quinn shrugged, saying nothing.

"There's one more thing," Sonny said carefully.

"What's that?"

"The neighbors on the other side of the building," Sonny said, referring to offices sharing a common wall with the bar, "they get a twenty-year lease for one dollar per year."

"Why would I agree to that?" Quinn's temper flared.

"Because they are a Catholic ministry, and I've never charged them rent. They do God's work. That's a deal breaker if you don't agree to it."

Quinn rolled her eyes. "God's work? Is that what you call it? Stork Ministries doesn't seem to do much from what I see."

"You don't see everything they do, but they take care of needs here and abroad," Sonny said. "They don't seek the limelight and go quietly about their work. God's work."

Quinn furled her brow while pushing her lips together, contemplating Sonny's conditions. Sonny turned his head and resumed staring out the window, waiting for the answer he knew would come.

"Okay, Sonny. Deal."

Sonny didn't move, didn't take his eyes away from the object of his gaze somewhere beyond the window. "I will have Bowerman prepare the documents; he will call you when they are ready for your signature."

"Okay," Quinn said. Realizing she had just been dismissed, she said nothing else but picked up her purse and left the dismal hospital room. Her mind raced as her steps quickened. She wanted to skip down the hospital hallway and share her news with everyone she passed. Her lips broke into a wide grin.

CHAPTER 34

"Is Sonny going to be here?" Eva asked.

"No, I'm just meeting with his attorney to sign the paperwork." Quinn pulled her Buick Century into a parking space. "But I appreciate you coming with me to help with this."

The women walked into Arnold Bowerman's office and checked in with the receptionist, then sat in the tiny, empty waiting room.

"When will all of this take effect?" Eva asked.

"Right away, as I understand it," Quinn said.

Soon a door opened and Bowerman stood there smiling with a manila file in hand. He invited Eva and Quinn to step into the adjoining conference room where he laid the folder on the smooth, dark, wood-grained table. Four chairs lined each side of the table and one was placed at each end. The chairs, with matching wood-stained arms, were cushioned in red leather. The paneled walls of the room dated it slightly, but also gave it a warm, rich feel. Nothing was out of place. This was clearly a room that had seen its share of deals made over the years.

The women sat on one side of the table while Bowerman sat at the end close to them. He opened the folder.

"Okay, Quinn. This is a big day for you, huh?" Bowerman sported a large set of perfectly white dentures, which looked out of place in his eighty-year-old face. His blue eyes sparkled.

Quinn smiled, unable to control herself. "I've always wanted to own my own business lock, stock, and barrel. This is a dream come true for me."

Eva slid her hand over and patted Quinn's forearm.

Bowerman placed a paper in front of Quinn and slid a pen toward her. The paper said *Quitclaim Deed* at the top.

"This is a Quitclaim Deed, showing that Mario Alvise Lupo II has relinquished his interest in the real estate and is passing it on to you. As you can see, the document has been lawfully witnessed by me." Bowerman looked at Quinn and then back down to the form, holding the tip of his ballpoint pen to the signature already affixed to the document. "You just need to sign right here, and then I'll have my legal secretary notarize it and make you a copy."

Quinn grinned and glanced briefly at Eva as she signed the document.

Bowerman picked up the document. "Wait here for a minute and I'll be right back," he said, exiting the room and closing the door behind him.

"I finally own something of my own." Quinn beamed. "I've dreamed of this, Eva. My life has been such a struggle for so long, and in the past year everything changed. I got you back, and now I have my own business. I actually own real estate!"

"I'm so proud of you, Mom. You deserve all of this. You deserve to be happy."

"I feel like I finally am somebody," Quinn spoke softly, folding her arms across her chest.

"You've always been somebody. Don't let anyone take that away from you. Most people couldn't go through what you have and survive, let alone be as successful as you have been."

Quinn's eyes filled with tears. For once, though, they were tears of happiness. She reached over and hugged Eva. "Thank you for being you," she said.

Quinn pulled back and looked at her daughter. "Owning the real estate is important not just because it's the first time I've ever owned property, but also because the liquor permit is a restricted permit," she said.

"What does that mean?" Eva asked.

"It means it's only good for that location and can never be transferred to another address. So it's important to have control of the physical property. If that property sold and the new owner didn't want to keep the bar open, the permit goes back to the state automatically, and it's no longer available for anyone to use. It has no value standing alone," Quinn explained. "Sonny doesn't think I know that, but I have known it all along."

Eva smiled at her mother. "You are sly!"

Quinn winked. "Just making sure my backside is covered."

After a few minutes Bowerman returned with paperwork in hand. "Okay, Quinn. Here is your copy of the deed. Keep it in a safe place."

He extended his hand to each woman as they stood to leave. "It's a pleasure doing business with you, ladies."

* * *

"You are a pretty remarkable woman," Eva said as Quinn eased the car onto the street from the parking lot.

"Why do you say that?" Quinn asked, surprised.

"When I think of everything you've been through, I am amazed at your resiliency and strength. How did you keep going forward?"

Quinn stopped the car at a red light and looked over at Eva, scanning her face. She looked back at the traffic light.

"I guess, as I look back on my life, I just did what came naturally for me," Quinn said thoughtfully. "I didn't know any other way, except to keep doing what I knew how to do and not being afraid to learn as I went along."

"But how did you not get overwhelmed with all the bullshit?"

"Oh, I did at times," Quinn said without hesitation. "I mean, there were times I wanted to give up. One time I tried. Thank God I wasn't successful. That suicide attempt scared the hell out of me and made me realize what I had to fight for … my kids as much as anything."

Quinn accelerated as traffic moved forward. Eva looked out the side window at the passing world, contemplating her mother's words.

"How did you not feel depressed all of the time? Especially when you were younger and had no options?" Eva asked.

"Who said I wasn't depressed? I lived with depression for a long time. I eventually figured out depression wasn't the problem."

"What do you mean?"

"Depression is the symptom of the problem. The real problem was my anger, my rage I kept bottled up inside me. Depression was just the way I contained the anger."

"So you're saying you dealt with your anger by being depressed?" Eva was skeptical.

"No, not dealt with it. Quite the opposite. My anger was dealing with me, in control of me. Depression was the way my mind handled it to keep me functioning on some level each day."

"Do you still get depressed?"

"No, not much," Quinn said. "Especially since you've come back to me. I will always feel guilty about giving you up, but at least the anger is gone now. For a long time I felt Douglas's death was God punishing me for giving you up."

"Really?" Eva was unable to conceal her surprise. "God doesn't work like that."

Quinn looked at Eva briefly, then back at the road. "I haven't yet figured out exactly how God does work, Eva. I probably will never fully understand him, but I do expect to see him someday, and I've got a lot of questions for him."

"Are you still angry with Sonny?"

"Angry? I wouldn't say that. He's not worth hating at this point in my life, but I certainly don't love him."

"So you're saying … what?" Eva asked.

"I only deal with him because I have to for business, but on a personal level, I neither hate nor love him, because both require energy. I am not a good enough person to will myself to love him. Ever. That would require me to forgive him, and I don't forgive him. That's God's job, not mine, as far as I'm concerned. But I am not willing to invest any emotional energy in him either."

"I've never thought of it that way," Eva said.

"I guess you could say the only thing worse than hating someone is to stop hating them and never love them. It reduces them to nothingness. I can tell you one thing for certain, though—"

"What's that?" Eva interrupted.

"When I stop hating, the anger stops. I am at peace. For the first time in my life, I am at peace with the world and, more importantly, with myself."

CHAPTER 35

1998

Quinn jumped at the ringing telephone in the dark bedroom. The digital clock on the bedside table displayed 4:43 in large, red numerals. She desperately groped for the phone, if not to answer it, then at least to shut it up. She propped herself on one elbow, pulling the receiver to her ear with her free hand.

"Hello?" Her throat was scratchy.

"Quinn?"

"Speaking, who is this?" Quinn didn't try to conceal her irritation.

"Serge DiPetro, Quinn."

"Oh, Serge. What's wrong?"

"It's the Prospector. It's on fire. It's bad. You need to get down there right now."

Quinn was fully awake now, swinging both her legs over the side of the bed as she sat up. "What happened?"

"I don't know, I am heading there now," DiPetro said. "Was anyone supposed to be in there tonight?"

"No, nobody," Quinn said. "We closed up at a few hours ago. Cleaning crew comes at six this morning. I locked up. It's empty."

"Okay, good. I will see you down there." DiPetro disconnected the call.

"What's going on?" Dave asked, sitting up in the bed.

"My bar is on fire!" Quinn hustled toward the bathroom. She frantically dressed, unconcerned about her appearance.

"I'll drive you." Dave grabbed his crumpled pants from the floor and pulled them on.

Fifteen minutes later, Quinn arrived at the Prospector to see the sky glowing orange as the building was fully engulfed. She looked at Dave as they sat on the front seat of the car and then back at the glowing building.

"It's gone," Quinn gasped. A lump formed in her throat. "There's nothing left for them to save."

Dave grabbed her hand and squeezed it. She pulled away as she lunged for the door handle. "I have to go see."

Dave interlocked his arm with Quinn's as they approached the barricade in the street. The police officer held out his hands and warned them not to come any closer.

"I'm the owner," Quinn said brusquely.

"Okay, Ma'am," the young officer said, "but it's not safe to get any closer right now."

Quinn said nothing, staring at the building, mesmerized by the flames. Her heart pounded, as she mentally processed the impact of the scene unfolding before her. What would she do? How could she ever replace everything inside that bar, the last eighteen years of her life?

"It's a building, Quinn. We'll rebuild it for you," Dave said softly.

"No, it's not just a building," Quinn said. "It's my life."

Dave put his arm around her and squeezed her tight, saying nothing more as Quinn continued to watch the devastation unfold before her. Slowly, as the fire hoses did their work, the flames were replaced with smoke—dark, thick, billowing smoke, as the streams of water fairly tickled the roaring beast, not putting it down but simply coaxing it into submission.

"It's going to be a total loss, Quinn." She looked away from the fire to see Serge DiPetro approaching her on the other side of the barricade. She couldn't react to those words. It was too much to process for her already overwhelmed mind.

"Any idea what could have caused this?" It was DiPetro again. Quinn looked at him, confused.

"What?" She then suddenly understood the implication. "Cause? Hell no! How would I know?"

"What I meant," DiPetro said, attempting to be tactful, "has anything changed recently—electrical work, remodeling, anything of that nature? Any appliances repaired?"

"No, nothing," Quinn said, looking at the charred building, flames now suppressed but smoke still rose from the heated structure.

"I would say that had to be more than an electrical fire," Dave spoke up. "She was just here and locked up around one-thirty, and everything was fine. It looks more like an explosion, gas leak, or something."

DiPetro shrugged, saying nothing. The young police officer walked over and motioned to DiPetro, who stepped away from Quinn and Dave. The two men spoke in low tones briefly.

"I have to go back over there," DiPetro said. "I'll let you know when I know something. Why don't you folks go home, get some coffee or some breakfast, and wait for me to call you? There's nothing you can do here right now. It's going to be later in the day before anything can be salvaged, but from the looks of it … there's nothing left to salvage anyway."

Dave led Quinn back to the car and drove her home. She showered as Dave made a pot of coffee and started making breakfast. A short time later, Quinn wandered into the kitchen wearing her bathrobe and a look of consternation.

"Something's fishy about this whole thing, Dave."

Dave looked up from the eggs crackling in the cast iron skillet. "Why do you say that?"

"Well, what could possibly have caused that kind of a fire so quickly?" Quinn sat down at the table as Dave put a cup of coffee in front of her.

"I don't know," Dave offered. "Let's just take it one step at a time. Let the police do their investigation and see what they come up with."

The phone rang, and Quinn grabbed the receiver from the wall of the kitchen. Dave listened to Quinn speak into the phone as he flipped the eggs over.

"Hello?"

"Yes?"

"When? Nine o'clock this morning? I'll be there."

She hung up the phone and looked at Dave.

"What?" he asked.

"That was the arson investigator. He wants to meet with me at the police station at nine." Quinn looked concerned.

"Arson?" Dave asked. "You're right. Something is fishy."

CHAPTER 36

"What do you mean, there's nothing left?" Eva gasped, putting her purse down on the kitchen table as she searched Quinn's face for answers.

"It was arson, and the insurance I thought I had is no good." Quinn's eyes were red, as bitter tears threatened to sear her cheeks yet again.

"How do you know this? Tell me what happened, from the beginning."

"I met with the arson investigator, and he was asking me all kinds of questions. It was clear he thought I had something to do with the fire."

"Okay, then what happened to change his mind?"

"After I was in there for over an hour, a detective comes in and shows the arson guy paperwork from the courthouse." Quinn started to cry again, futilely wiping at her eyes with her handkerchief. "It turns out, I don't even own the property."

"What?" Eva exclaimed. "I was with you—you have the deed!"

"Yeah, well, old Bowerman pulled a fast one on us, apparently," Quinn stopped to blow her nose.

"How so?" Eva was impatient for information.

"First of all, the quitclaim deed, do you remember that?"

"Yes," Eva said. "Sort of. I remember us going there to sign it, but I didn't pay much attention to the deed. What about it?"

"It was never recorded with the county. Bowerman never recorded it, so there's no documentation that Sonny ever signed it over to me. Turns out, even if he had recorded it, it's invalid because there has to be two witnesses to the signatures. There was only one. Bowerman knew what he was doing, and Sonny is behind all this." Quinn shook her head before resting her forehead in her hands, elbows on the table.

"What about insurance ... what did you say about that?" Eva asked.

"Sonny handled that. Said he transferred the policy to me, even showed me papers with my name on it."

"What company? Have you talked to the agent?"

"Eva, no, don't you get it?" Quinn said, looking at her daughter. "It wasn't a legitimate insurance company. Sonny faked those documents. I never should have let him handle that. It just seemed easier at the time."

"So if you don't legally own the property, who does?" Eva tried to piece everything together.

"Lark Enterprises, Incorporated."

"Who's that?"

"I don't know, but when I was at the police station there was an IRS investigator there, and he was the one asking the most questions about Lark Enterprises. I don't know if he believed me or not when I told him I'd never heard of them."

Eva thought for a few minutes, then looked at Quinn.

"I know who has the answers to all of this, Mom."

Quinn looked at her, knowing what she was going to say.

"Yeah, I know ... Sonny," Quinn said, resignation in her voice. "All trails always lead back to him. But since his second heart attack, he can hardly get out of bed, from what I've been told."

"Do you believe that?" Eva asked.

"I don't know what to believe anymore," Quinn said, dejectedly. "All I know is that I have nothing—no business, no real estate, and no insurance money. I am wiped out. And I'm too old to recover from this financially."

"So you didn't have insurance, but I'll bet Lark Enterprises did, don't you think?" Eva said.

"Probably so. Someone burned it down for a reason, and I'm sure it was for money."

"I guarantee you Sonny is behind this," Eva said, standing up. "I'm going to go to his house and confront him."

"Wait, Eva, don't! Nothing good will come of that."

"I'm not afraid of him," Eva said, her eyes snapping. "It's time someone took something away from him."

Eva stormed out of the house before Quinn could stop her. She watch as Eva's car screeched out of the driveway. Quinn grabbed her purse and searched for her car keys. She had to stop Eva before something happened they'd both regret.

CHAPTER 37

"Why are you here?" Sonny's voice was tired, his large frame stretched out on the bed. He looked substantially thinner than the last time the priest had seen him.

"Why, to comfort you in your hour of need," Father Schaefer said.

"You can't comfort me."

Schaefer smiled as he stood beside the bed, looking down on Sonny.

"Sit down! Don't just stand there looking at me," Sonny grumbled.

The old priest shuffled over to a chair and sat, saying nothing. The two men shared the silence for several minutes, as was their habit.

"A lot has happened in the past week," Schaefer said.

"Yes. We've been purified by fire. They cannot refute our claim that everything was lost in the fire. Our records problem just vanished."

"You know, it's not too late to seek God's mercy," Schaefer offered.

Sonny chuckled, turning his head to look at the priest. "Maybe it's too early."

"You've always been an optimist, Sonny."

"If you don't believe in the bright possibilities of tomorrow, you stay stuck in today forever."

"That's profound. And slightly poetic."

"So tell me, Father," Sonny started, "do you think God is going to magically make a place in heaven for me?"

"Yes. But it's not magic."

Sonny laughed derisively.

Schaefer shrugged. "Laugh all you want. You're missing the deal of a lifetime."

"It makes no sense. It never has made sense. We do what we do, us human beings, and no matter what we do, God gives us a pass."

"In essence, yes, that's right."

"What about that makes sense to you? If there are rules, and you violate the rules, but there's no penalty for violating the rules, then what's the point of the rules?"

"I never said there's no penalty," Schaefer corrected Sonny.

"Yeah, I know, we spend time in purgatory, the penalty box, but in the end, we live with God forever, no matter what, as long as we are baptized, play by the church rules, and confess our sins before we die. I taught all my kids that, but I never thought it made a lot of sense."

"If that's how you feel, then why does it bother you? If you think there is no God, why not just forget it all?" Schaefer challenged.

"I didn't say there was no God. I just think he's a bastard."

"Perhaps, Sonny, your God is a bastard. I don't know. My God is not."

"Maybe you will think otherwise when you stand before him," Sonny said.

"Perhaps, but it's doubtful. I have been an instrument of his peace and done his good work faithfully. I have devoted my life to him, and he will be pleased with me."

Sonny raised his head, looking at the old priest. "My God, you really believe that, don't you?"

"Of course. Why would I say it if I didn't believe it?"

"You sanctimonious sonofabitch," Sonny said. "You think you are better than me, don't you?"

"Why quibble over such things? God will sort it out. But I will say that I, unlike you, have never deviated from the will of God. Of that I am certain. I have done his will, and even though I haven't always understood the 'why,' I didn't question. I am a good servant of my Lord. That counts for a lot."

Sonny laid his head back down on the pillow. "Do you think God wanted you to do all of the things you have done?"

"Yes, I know he wanted me to help all the people I have helped. You were part of that, you know. It was a good thing we did for all those families. God is pleased."

"And you don't question whether it was right or wrong?" Sonny asked.

"In the book of Romans, we learn God's judgments are unsearchable and his ways unknowable."

"So then, you don't know you did God's work, do you?"

"When we have deep faith, we hear the voice of God speaking to us. After all these years, you still do not understand, do you? The real difference between us?"

"What's that?"

"The depth of our faith. I have a strong faith, and I am in constant communion with my Lord. You, on the other hand, attempt to use the Lord for your own purposes, covering up your sin with your holiness. But be assured, when you fail to do the Lord's will, you have sinned, and your sin will find you out."

"Don't you believe God knows all?"

"Of course," Schaefer replied. "Of course."

"Then don't you think he knows your true heart? He knows your true thoughts? Your true motivations?"

Schaefer stood up slowly, looking calmly at Sonny.

"I absolutely do. That's why I know I will be with him in heaven someday." Schaefer studied Sonny's expressionless face. "Now I have a question for you."

Sonny said nothing but simply raised his eyebrows.

"Soon, you will be far away from this place. Soon, you will be in a different world from all this, the trappings of your life here. Are you ready for that?"

CHAPTER 38

Eva stopped abruptly, parking at the curb in front of Sonny's house. Darkness was just setting in. She had calmed down enough to think, but not enough to think rationally. She opened her purse and looked at the five-shot, snub-nose revolver. Could she do this? She was afraid of the answer and didn't intend to spend any more time thinking about it. She just wanted to see his face, the look in his eyes, when she pointed the gun at his head. She jumped out of the car, walking around the back of it just as she saw the old priest emerging from the house. She heard a car door slam and turned around to see her mother scrambling across the street.

"Eva, wait! Let me talk to you!" Panic was apparent in Quinn's face and voice.

Eva faced her mother. "Go back home. I will handle this."

"No, it's not what I want." Quinn protested.

Father Schaefer approached Eva. She looked directly at him, his face clear in the illumination of the yard light, his expression peculiar. Quinn sidled up to Eva, placing her hand on Eva's shoulder.

Schaefer looked at them both. "You're too late. He's gone."

ACKNOWLEDGMENTS

I want to thank my husband, children, and grandchildren, who make my life complete. And to the Universe for pulling the cooperative components together after twenty years and introducing me to Mike Blass, who is the word person for my big picture.

—Erin Walsh Hardesty

The limitations of space and memory preclude me from acknowledging all of the people who have informed and enriched my life for nearly six decades. Yet, without question, those whose choices have impacted my life have made my contributions to this project possible. Some did so through a conscious choice to teach, mentor, or coach. Many more did so by choosing to live their lives in a way that exemplified behaviors that I aspire to emulate. Still others who choose to provide perspective, love, and support through meaningful friendships and family relationships. We are the product of choices—our own and others'. For that, and for those people in my life, I am grateful.

—Michael Blass

We would like to thank the following people who have contributed substantially to our work on this, our very first book. Each of you have left an indelible mark on our project, and we are honored that you were willing to be a part of our effort. Our editor, Christi McGuire, provided valuable advice and guidance as we navigated the literary and publishing world. Her insights, her expertise, and her patience are unrivaled! Matt Potter worked tirelessly on our cover design until we felt we had it "just right." We sincerely appreciate the input and feedback provided by Keith Bicknell, Marlin Kirkendall, Jodie Neal, and Paige Townsend prior to final editing; each of you chose to freely give of your time to help us, and we are grateful.

—Erin Walsh Hardesty and Michael Blass

ABOUT THE AUTHORS

Erin Walsh Hardesty is the biological daughter of the real-life person upon which Quinn O'Connell's character is based. She was born in Norfolk, Virginia, and three days later her adoptive parents brought her to Lima, Ohio, where she was born and raised and still resides. Erin has been sharing her true-life experience of finding her birthmother with audiences since 1992. She is active in her community and has worked in the financial services industry for thirty-five years.

Michael Blass has written extensively throughout his thirty-year career in government service. Retired in 2008, Mike has established multiple business interests with his sons in the construction and real-estate sectors. Since 1995 he has been the owner of Michael A. Blass & Associates, consulting for a wide variety of public-sector organizations on a range of topics.

Erin and Mike have partnered to form No Little Choices, LLC, a consulting company that educates individuals and organizations about the power of choice in personal and professional development. They are currently working on additional novels as sequels to *No Little Choices,* as part of the *sherrilrose* series. Erin and Mike have developed the *3 Dimensions of Personal Power: A Practical Guide to Living Life Powerfully and Vibrantly* and are collaborating on a nonfiction book by the same name.

To schedule Erin and Mike for speaking engagements, please visit www.NoLittleChoices.com.

The following is excerpt from the sequel of *No Little Choices*, releasing in Summer 2017.

Sonny

CHAPTER 1

1934
Calabria, Italy

Eight-year-old Sonny heard and felt the sting of his mother's right hand before his eyes detected any movement. His cheek screamed with heat as the reality of the moment finally seeped into his brain.

"Never say that about your father," his mother spit the words into Sonny's face, her dark eyes alive with fire, her mouth contorted angrily with each syllable.

Sonny said nothing. Tears filled his eyes. His legs trembled. His gaze dropped to the floor.

"Look at me!" Mama's words jerked him back from his momentary retreat. He felt her hard hands on his shoulders and looked up into her burning onyx eyes.

"Why would you lie about such a thing? Why would you make up such a vile lie about your father? "

"But it's not a lie, Mama—"

Mama's hand enveloped Sonny's chin and cheeks in a vice-like grip, pushing his cheeks into his teeth. "Shut your mouth! I will whip you for the sins you commit, Mario. No more, do you hear?" With each word her hand seemed to tighten a little more. Sonny's lips were smooshed together so tightly he was unable to open them. He stood on his tippy-toes as his mother pulled at his tender face with her strong hands. She wore an ugly, unfamiliar mask. Sonny felt fear shoot out from his belly into his toes and up into his head.

"And what about Sophia? You bring shame to talk about your sister in this way!"

Sonny said nothing as Mama's face softened only slightly, her hand slowly relaxing as she held her gaze into his eyes. Sonny saw her nostrils flare slightly as the muscles in her jaws flexed. Her eyes changed, the fire extinguished, replaced by two dark and dull orbs partially hidden under half-closed eyelids. She dropped her hand calmly, almost gently.

"You must go to confession," she said flatly, as she slowly turned away from Sonny.

Sonny didn't respond and slowly moved toward the door, unsure what to do next but instinctively knowing he should leave his mother's presence.

"Sonny," Mama's voice was quiet now, as she stood facing the wall, her back to him.

Sonny looked up and stared at the back of her head. "Yes?" he whispered.

"Never again will you speak of this. This is between you and the priest and God now. And nobody else. Understand?"

"Yes, Mama."

She turned slightly to look at Sonny for emphasis. Their eyes met. "We don't speak of our sins."

"Yes, Mama."

READING GROUP DISCUSSION QUESTIONS

Chapter 1

1. Who is controlling the situation in this chapter?
2. Who has the most power—Sonny or Quinn? Is either person powerless?
3. Discuss what power means to you. How do you define it?

Chapter 2

1. Grandma attempts to discourage Quinn from helping the baby bird. Why?
2. Why does Quinn seem to be enamored with the baby bird?
3. Quinn refers to an argument between her mother and Sonny as the reason she was sent to live with Grandma. What might have led to this conflict?

Chapter 3

1. Roxanna is adamant that Quinn divulge the name of the baby's father. Why?
2. Roxanna sees defiance in her daughter's eyes, while Grandma sees pain. Who do you most relate to? Explain.
3. Why would Quinn refuse to divulge Sonny as the father of her baby?
4. What are Grandma's expectations of Roxanna? How might this affect Roxanna's behavior, if at all?

Chapter 4

1. Quinn is reluctant to release the bird, even after Grandma explains that it will die if not set free. Why does Quinn find it so difficult to release the bird? Discuss her motivations.
2. Discuss the concept of risk as it relates to Grandma's statement that Quinn must "let nature take its course." How does risk impact our ability to learn and grow?
3. Grandma tells Quinn that life is a game of give and take and that "the why doesn't matter." Do you agree with this? Why or why not?

Chapter 5

1. "Quinn knew [Sonny] well … better than he knew himself." What do you think this means? How do our "blind spots" (those things others know about us that we don't know about ourselves) affect our personal development?
2. Quinn acquiesces to Sonny's instructions. Why is she so compliant?
3. Discuss how Quinn exercises personal power in this chapter.
4. At chapter's end, Sonny refers to Quinn as a "little slut." What conscious and/or subconscious thoughts might drive this comment?

Chapter 6

1. Do you believe Quinn is intimidated by the priest? What leads you to your conclusion?
2. Pretend you are Quinn in the moments immediately after your encounter with Father Schaeffer. Describe your observations and feelings about the priest.
3. What is the source of Father Schaeffer's power? How does he exercise this power?
4. We communicate our core values through our thoughts, words, and actions. What do you think Father Schaeffer's core values are, based on his conversation with Quinn?
5. During her interaction with Father Schaeffer, Quinn faces many decision points. Identify the choices she made throughout the conversation and discuss her possible motivations for each choice.
6. Why do you think Father Schaeffer asked Quinn who the baby's father was? Do you think he was surprised that she refused to tell?
7. How does gender factor into the power dynamic between Quinn and Father Schaeffer? Age? Life experience?

Chapter 7

1. What does the robin at the window symbolize?
2. What parallels can be drawn between Aunt Peggy's perspective on crocheting and Quinn's situation?
3. Identify one core value evidenced by Aunt Peggy's comments. In other words, name one thing that is important to Aunt Peggy

and defines how she sees herself fitting into the world.

4. Aunt Peggy tells Quinn "the best thing we can do for ourselves … is to create something beautiful and give it away." How do we benefit by giving? Do you suppose Aunt Peggy had a deeper meaning for Quinn in this statement?

Chapter 8

1. Why is Roxanna being deceptive with Peggy?
2. Compare and contrast the motives of Roxanna and Peggy, as related to Quinn.
3. How does self-interest impact the circumstances described in the phone conversation between Roxanna and Peggy?
4. How does Roxanna use Peggy's blind spot to manipulate her sister?
5. Of the two sisters, who is more acutely aware of the other's mindset, thinking, and motivations? How does this relate to each sister's personal power?
6. Was Roxanna actively complicit in the surreptitious plot to have Quinn's baby brought back to Ohio? Explain what might be motivating her to behave in this fashion.
7. Roxanna "had little patience for [Peggy's] irritating way of being bright and cheerful." Why would Roxanna react with irritation?

Chapter 9

1. What is Tom Grady referring to when he talks about insurance?
2. Based on Tom's conversation with Sonny, what can you determine about Sonny's choices in life?
3. Based on what you know about Sonny thus far, describe one of his likely core values.

Chapter 10

1. Why does Father Schaeffer register surprise when Sonny says he has a "sister in need"?
2. What critical choices has Sonny made in life that have resulted in his current situation?
3. The priest and Sonny "neither loved nor hated one another." Explain the dynamics of a relationship devoid of both love and hate.
4. Father Schaeffer seems to recognize a character flaw in Sonny.

What is it? Do you think Sonny views this as a weakness or a strength?

5. What is Father Schaeffer's motivation for pointing out Sonny's blind spot?
6. Describe the balance of power between Sonny and Father Schaeffer. What is the source of each man's power?

Chapter 11

1. What role does gender play in this chapter? How does it influence the actions of Sonny? Serge? Roxanna?
2. Describe a situation in which your gender worked against you.
3. Describe a situation in which your gender worked in your favor.
4. Why did Serge provide Sonny with the Ralph Waldo Emerson quote?
5. Roxanna displays a range of emotions, including anger. Aside from Karen, who is Roxanna's anger directed toward? Why?

Chapter 12

1. Sonny tells Quinn to go to confession. Explain your theory as to why this has become a part of his ritual when sexually abusing Quinn.
2. Two years have passed since Quinn left home to have her baby. Now she is back in the same situation. Based upon her interactions with Sonny, how has Quinn changed?
3. Dreams are an expression of our subconscious mind at work. What can you determine about Quinn's perception of her place in the world, based upon the events she dreamed about?

Chapter 13

1. As Bonnie and Quinn discuss childbirth, Bonnie giggles. Why does Quinn become annoyed? How might their different life experiences affect their sense of priorities and/or values?
2. What emotions and thoughts might Quinn be experiencing as she learns that Charlie Freund is interested in her? If you put yourself in Quinn's shoes at this moment, how do you think you would react? What would you fear?
3. Why does Quinn say, "I let them take my baby away"? Discuss the implications of her perspective on the adoption. How has this

affected her? How might her perspective affect her life going forward?

4. What stands in the way of Quinn being able to move on and forget the baby she gave up?
5. How has this experience affected Quinn's self-image? Her relationship with God?
6. Quinn expresses her view that she "has a hole in her soul and there is no place in heaven for a soul that is not whole." Assuming that our damaged souls are a result of sin, and all human beings sin, are some sins worse than others? Explain.

Chapter 14

1. Based upon her conversation with Quinn, how would you describe Roxanna's value system? What is most important to her?
2. Why does Quinn find imperfections in herself, even as she "stood there, flawless"?
3. How would Quinn describe "the real Quinn"? Why?
4. In her attempts to convince Quinn to go to the prom, Roxanna communicates a deeper message about Quinn. What is it? What could cause Roxanna to say these things?

Chapter 15

1. Based upon Quinn's retelling of Charlie's conversation with Sonny and her mother, describe Quinn's sense of belonging in her family. What subtle message does Quinn receive? How might this affect her sense of self?
2. Why is Quinn so willing to rationalize Charlie's illegal activity?
3. What is the balance of power between Quinn and Bonnie? Who is dominant in the relationship? What benefit does each person receive from being in the relationship? What does each person provide to the other that feeds their friendship?
4. Bonnie and Quinn are different in many ways. Think about the life experiences, value system, and personality of each girl. Can you explain why they think and act the way they do? Which girl are you most like? How so?

Chapter 16

1. Charlie uses Quinn to arrange a meeting with Sonny. What is Charlie's motivation for doing so? Why does Quinn agree to this? How does Charlie manipulate Quinn?
2. How does Quinn manipulate Charlie?
3. In your opinion, what is Quinn seeking in life at this point? What emotional need is she attempting to fill? What does Charlie seek?

Chapter 17

1. The triggering event of Roxanna's suicide attempt was Sonny's affair with Karen. What was Roxanna's motivation?
2. Identify the people who were affected by Roxanna's choice to attempt suicide and how her attempt might have impacted them.
3. Why is Quinn so curious about the family at O'Banyon's market? What might this family represent to her?
4. When Bonnie registers surprise that Roxanna doesn't want to leave Sonny, Quinn replies "It doesn't work that way." What do you think Quinn is referring to?

Chapter 18

1. Why does Sonny instruct Quinn to say nothing to the police? Does Quinn comply?
2. Why did Quinn bait Sonny after the cops searched her home?
3. How has the balance of power changed between Quinn and Sonny? Do each of them retain the same amount of power in the relationship that each of them had when Quinn was 13? Explain the reasons for any change you've observed.
4. Do you think Quinn is afraid of Sonny? Why or why not?
5. What, in your opinion, is Quinn's view of Sonny? How do you think she would describe their relationship at this point?
6. Is Quinn intimidated by the police when they come to her home? Why or why not? What is your impression of Quinn's perspective on authority? What influences her perspective?

Chapter 19

1. Sonny orchestrated Charlie's "confession" and subsequent stiff jail sentence, yet Charlie still trusts Sonny. Explain the dynamics of the relationship between Sonny and Charlie, based upon what

you know about the characters at this point.
2. List the choices Sonny and Charlie have made that have caused them to be in their current situation. Consider not only recent choices, but past choices as well.
3. How have Sonny and Charlie's individual choices affected each of them? How have those choices affected the other person in the relationship? How have these choices affected the balance of power in the relationship?
4. Is the relationship between Sonny and Charlie mutually beneficial? Why or why not?

Chapter 20

1. Sonny seems cavalier in his attitude toward Quinn, as he continues his manipulation and control. Quinn becomes more confrontational. Discuss the changing interpersonal dynamic occurring between them. Do you think the relationship is purely pragmatic—that is, one driven by necessity and serving a utilitarian purpose? Or is it more complicated than that? Explain.
2. In his conversation with Quinn, Sonny refers to himself as her father. What do you think his motivations are for saying this? Do you think he sees himself as a father figure to Quinn?
3. Do you think Sonny's comments about his sexual relationship with Quinn are sincere or simply a way to rationalize his behavior? If you were Sonny's advocate and were forced to explain the root causes of his sexual abuse of Quinn, what possible factors might you consider?
4. Why might Quinn have lingering doubt about her own role in these events?

Chapter 21

1. Quinn encounters Father Schaeffer at the hospital. What can you infer about their perception of one another from their brief conversation?
2. Discuss how the power dynamic has changed significantly between Quinn and Sonny. Is it fair to say that Quinn is acting in her own self-interest and exploiting Sonny's condition and circumstance to gain advantage? In your opinion, is Quinn right or wrong for doing this? Explain.

3. What adjectives would you use to describe Quinn at this point in her life?
4. At the end of the chapter, Sonny asks Quinn, "Why?" He appears confused and emotional. In your opinion, is this genuine? Why or why not?
5. Discuss the choices both Quinn and Sonny make in this encounter and how those choices affect the other person.

Chapter 22

1. Why does Quinn become physically ill immediately after visiting Sonny?
2. Why does Quinn miss "the world of familiar misery she had just left behind" as she walked from Sonny's room to leave the hospital? What is significant about this experience?
3. What changed within Quinn after she sits in the hot car in the hospital parking lot for fifteen minutes?
4. After leaving the hospital, Quinn goes to O'Banyon's market to shop. Why does she become annoyed with the comment made by the little girl, "I'm white, I'm Catholic, and nobody in my family is divorced"?

Chapter 23

1. Based upon their conversation at the railyard, briefly describe the perspectives of Sonny and Charlie relative to gender equality and their views of women in general.
2. Charlie seems to be braced for conflict with Quinn over Sonny's management of the bar. Instead, Quinn readily complies with Charlie's "edict." We then discover that Quinn is pregnant. Do you think Quinn would have reacted differently if she were not pregnant? Why or why not?
3. If you put yourself in Quinn's place, having run the bar profitably and successfully for five years, how would you react if told you had to give up your job? How did the power of choice factor into Quinn's reaction?

Chapter 24

1. Eva and Jennifer have grown from two little girls playing in a grocery store into talented teenagers who are active in their church. Both girls appear to be infatuated with Mr. Lupo. Do

you think Mr. Lupo is aware of this? How would you describe his interactions with the girls?

2. Mr. Lupo carefully explains the significance of the pelican referenced in the song that they rehearse. Why would he take the time to do this? Based on what you know about him, describe Mr. Lupo's character and a core value.
3. All religions use the power of symbolism, myth, and storytelling to convey key tenants of their faith to their followers. Mr. Lupo explains the meaning of the pelican and its symbolism, yet at the end of the conversation he says, "It really doesn't matter how a pelican feeds her babies." Does the use of myth and symbolism in religion serve to strengthen or weaken one's ability to believe? Explain.
4. Does the "power to choose" impact one's ability to believe?

Chapter 25

1. All choices have consequences—some large, some small. Identify the decision points and the consequence of each choice made by the characters in this chapter.
2. Compare and contrast the reactions of the girls and Mrs. Freund after one of the children utters the profane word. What is significant about Mrs. Freund's reaction? Eva's reaction? Jennifer's reaction?
3. What choices do each of them make during their brief conversation?

Chapter 26

1. Douglas was an eight-year-old boy struggling with a basket of peaches as he attempted to help his mother by following her instructions. He was innocently doing the right thing, yet he was killed in an instant. What does this teach us about life's inequities? About the power of choice? About consequences?
2. As Jennifer struggles to process the trauma she has just witnessed, her thoughts turn to how she ended up in this place at this time: "I just wanted to make extra money this summer." It is almost as if she is rationalizing her own actions. Why does Jennifer have this fleeting thought? How does it assist her in processing the terrible thing she has unavoidably witnessed? How does the power of choice relate to Jennifer's situation in this moment?

3. If you were Linda, the boys' mother, what would you say to Jennifer to help her deal with her feelings?

Chapter 27

1. Mr. Lupo attempts to calm Jennifer and Eva and shows concern for their well-being. He says that "life is not fair." Do you agree with his assessment? Do you feel that life's unfairness works for or against you?
2. Compare and contrast Mr. Lupo's and Father Schaeffer's comments. Which man would you prefer to have at your side when grieving?
3. Mr. Lupo tells Eva and Jennifer that they can have a better understanding of God's will if they so choose. Can our ability to exercise choice immediately and directly change what we are feeling? Explain.

Chapter 28

1. Do you think Father Schaeffer's words during the funeral service were words of comfort to Douglas's mother? Why or why not? Do you think church orthodoxy sometimes impede understanding and healing? How so?
2. What choices might Mrs. Freund make in her life that will promote the healing process as she grieves over the loss of her son?
3. Jennifer seems to have an unspoken opinion about the funeral service. If she spoke candidly, what do you think she might say? Why?
4. Why might Mr. Freund feel compelled to blame Mrs. Freund for Douglas's death? What conscious or subconscious thoughts could drive this behavior?
5. Aside from the obvious loss of Douglas, why would Jennifer say, "that family seems to have a lot of problems"? Explain how this thinking might help Jennifer make sense of and cope with the loss of Douglas.

Chapter 29

1. Describe Quinn's view of God. Do you agree or disagree with her?
2. Quinn is riddled with guilt throughout much of her adult life up

to this point. Do you think her feelings are justified? Why or why not? What advice would you give her to help her cope with her guilt?

3. How does Quinn's experience with Sonny, at a very young age, impact Quinn's view of God? Does gender play a role in this?

Chapter 30

1. When Quinn answered the phone and was asked about giving birth to a child in 1954, she could easily have lied. Why do you think she chose to answer truthfully? Discuss her possible motives.
2. Why does Eva make a point of correcting Quinn's use of the term "adoptive parents"? What emotions might Eva be experiencing?
3. List the risks each woman faces as they consider forging a relationship. What motivations might each of them have to face these risks?
4. When Quinn and Eva first meet face to face, they embrace for several minutes. Do you believe two people could bond so quickly, with so few spoken words between them? Why or why not?
5. How might your life experiences affect your answer to Question #4 above?

Chapter 31

1. Eva was shocked when she discovered the identity of her biological father. She struggles to reconcile the Sonny Lupo that Quinn describes with the Mr. Lupo she knew growing up in the church. Which version of Lupo do you think is the most accurate? Why?
2. Assuming everything Quinn said about Sonny is true, why would he choose to be active in the church? Do you believe he could serve a purpose—man or God's—by being active in the church? Explain.
3. Quinn tells Eva her perspective on survival: "Sometimes you have to wallow with the hogs and suffer the shit before you can eat the bacon." What does she mean? How does the power of choice come into play? Do you agree with her?
4. Based on her life experiences, accomplishments, and ideas, would you describe Quinn as an optimist or a pessimist? Do you

think her perspective has been a strength or a weakness? Explain.

5. Quinn demonstrates a keen understanding of Sonny, perhaps knowing more about him than he knows about himself. Do you think it is important to understand another person's emotional needs (those things that cause behavior, motivations, etc.) in order to maintain a positive relationship with that person? Explain.

Chapter 32

1. Sonny asks Quinn if she can forgive him for abusing her when she was young. She refuses to do so. How might Quinn's refusal affect Sonny? How might it affect her? Do you think she should have forgiven him? Why or why not?
2. Sonny at first denies having any involvement in Eva's return to and adoption in Louiston. He quickly concedes his involvement and claims that he wanted to make sure she was okay growing up. Do you think he was being sincere? Why or why not? Do you think Sonny fully understood the impact the adoption had on Quinn? Explain.
3. Quinn faces a critical decision point when she realizes Sonny is unconscious and likely dying in front of her. She is tempted to allow him to die, yet she doesn't. As he is taken away by the EMTs, Quinn "resigned herself to the fact that Sonny might survive." Why is Quinn so conflicted? In your opinion, what caused Quinn to make the choices she made?

Chapter 33

1. What is Quinn's motivation for talking to Sonny about his legacy?
2. Explain Quinn's feelings for Sonny—positive, negative, or ambivalent? Why does Quinn continue to interact with Sonny, instead of severing all ties?
3. Do you think Quinn was justified in negotiating a business deal with Sonny when he was in a weakened state, both physically and emotionally? Why or why not?

Chapter 34

1. Why was Quinn so excited about owning something of her very own? What might the official ownership of a business mean to

her? How might it affect her self-image?

2. What does Quinn's life teach us about resiliency and persistence? Has there been a time in your life when you prevailed after a long struggle when outcome was uncertain? How did you persevere?
3. Quinn refers to another characteristic that she credits for her success. What is it? Explain how this characteristic and persistence are linked.
4. Quinn tells Eva that her depression "was the way my mind handled [my anger] to keep me functioning ... each day." What does she mean? Do you agree? How does our power to choose impact our ability to handle anger? Depression?
5. Quinn has an insight into the correlation between love, hate, anger, and peace. Do you agree with her assessment that the only thing "worse than hating someone is to stop hating them … It reduces them to nothingness"? Explain.

Chapter 35

1. Quinn watches her life's dream literally go up in smoke before her eyes. What thoughts do you think were racing through her mind?
2. How did Quinn's power of choice affect her actions as she watched the burning building?
3. What emotions do you think Quinn felt as she watched this destruction? How did she handle those emotions?

Chapter 36

1. Quinn has discovered that she has no insurance to cover the loss of the building, and she appears defeated and dejected. Eva, on the other hand, is angry and decides to confront Sonny. Quinn attempts to dissuade her. Why?

2. Quinn pursues Eva. What does this say about Quinn's priorities at this point in her life?

Chapter 37

1. Father Schaeffer says that Sonny has always been an optimist, and Sonny responds by saying, "If you don't believe in the bright possibilities of tomorrow, you may stay stuck in today forever."

What does he mean by this? Do you agree?

2. In your opinion, do we choose to be either optimistic or pessimistic, or is our disposition part of the genetics we inherit from our parents?
3. Sonny tells Father Schaeffer that God is "a bastard." Why would Sonny say this?
4. Father Schaeffer says he has devoted his life to God and that God will be pleased with him on his judgement day. Do you think Schaeffer is correct, based upon what you know about him at this point? Why or why not?
5. Sonny sees Father Schaeffer far differently than Father Schaeffer sees himself, yet these men have known each other for decades. How can this be?

Chapter 38

1. Who has stronger feelings for Sonny—Quinn or Eva? Explain.
2. Why does Quinn say, "It's not what I want," when Eva indicated she was going to confront Sonny? How does motherhood affect Quinn's thinking at this point?
3. According to Father Schaeffer, Sonny is gone. What choices now face Eva, relative to the emotions she is feeling toward Sonny? Can she use the power of choice to find peace? Explain.
4. Our legacy manifests the power and vibrancy of our lives, and it allows us to touch the lives of those who knew us and those who never will. Based on what you know about Quinn, what is her legacy? Sonny?